PEN[illegible] BOOKS

SHA[illegible]

Robert Marshall [illegible]
He graduated fro[illegible]
1973. Since 1980 [illegible]
BBC History Unit and among [illegible]
First Spymaster, *The Black Death*, *The Tories and the Working Class*, *All the King's Men*, *The Marble Hunter*, *The Zulu Wars*, *Light in the Dark* and *Summer of the Bomb*. He is also author of television plays and a number of books, including *All the King's Men* (1987), *The Sewers of Lvov* (1990) and a novel, *The Constant Spy* (1990).

Shadow Makers

A NOVEL BY

ROBERT MARSHALL

BASED ON THE SCREENPLAY BY

BRUCE ROBINSON

AND

ROLAND JOFFE

STORY BY

BRUCE ROBINSON

PENGUIN BOOKS

PENGUIN BOOKS

Published by the Penguin Group
27 Wrights Lane, London W8 5TZ, England
Viking Penguin Inc., 40 West 23rd Street, New York, New York 10010, USA
Penguin Books Australia Ltd, Ringwood, Victoria, Australia
Penguin Books Canada Ltd, 2801 John Street, Markham, Ontario, Canada L3R 1B4
Penguin Books (NZ) Ltd, 182–190 Wairau Road, Auckland 10, New Zealand

Penguin Books Ltd, Registered Offices: Harmondsworth, Middlesex, England

Published in Penguin Books 1990
10 9 8 7 6 5 4 3 2 1

Filmset in Lasercomp Plantin

Made and printed in Great Britain by
Richard Clay Ltd, Bungay, Suffolk

ONE

The fat man slumped deep into the back seat of the cab and waited as it crawled into the mid-morning traffic on Wabash Avenue. Nobody seemed to be getting anywhere, so he reached for another Hershey Bar from the bag in his coat pocket and resigned himself to perusing the scenery. He was not someone who spent much time gazing out of windows. Travelling time was usually maximized by going through reports or reading the news from Europe. His plump hand caressed the old leather briefcase at his side and eventually slipped the lock. He took out the buff-coloured file he'd studied on the train from Washington and decided to run through the highlights again.

He glanced at the name – SZILARD – typed along the leading edge and rehearsed his pronunciation of another of those damned unpronounceable middle-European names.

'Hungarian,' he declared to himself, as if it were something quite unpardonable.

'Nuclear Physicist. Studied under Einstein. Ph.D. from the Kaiser Wilhelm Institute. Left Berlin, 1933.'

There was a copy of a patent, taken out by Szilard in London during 1934, describing how a nuclear chain-reaction would work. Attached to it was a letter from the British War Office stating they could find 'no reason why this specification should be kept secret'. The fat man groaned as he fell on those words again. At the back of the file was a copy of a proposal from the Hungarian to the President of the United States of America, dated August 1939 and signed by Albert Einstein. The fat man scanned the proposal, picking out the salient details.

It predicted that it would be 'conceivable' to produce 'extremely powerful bombs of a new type'. It went on to describe the progress the Germans were making on the same idea and urged the president to get America committed to developing the 'chain-reaction' bomb as soon as possible. On another page was a copy and translation of a secret report to the German War Office in Berlin from a scientist in Hamburg. Dated 24 April 1939, it read in part: '. . . will probably make it possible to produce an explosive ten times more powerful than conventional ones'. Then the show-stopper: 'The country that first makes use of it has an unsurpassable advantage over the others.'

Those last, key words had burned themselves in the fat man's conscience. It was September 1942. If the Germans were already three years ahead then the whole exercise might be a waste of time. He flipped back to the front of the file and read that Szilard was now part of a group of scientists at the University of Chicago working on a large-scale experiment to prove that an atomic chain-reaction was possible. Latest reports did not reckon they were making great progress.

The fat man heaved himself out of the cab and ploughed into the hotel lobby. As the cage door closed on the elevator, he jabbed the button for the eleventh floor. He distrusted academics. 'Eggheads' and 'long-hairs' he called them. Dry, tedious – pencil-pushers who had no real grasp of priorities. Priorities: that was the essence of his world.

As the steel contraption rose slowly past each floor, briefly illuminating a little of the structure of the old pile, he allowed himself to be carried back to a month before – to a world where he felt much more comfortable. Where he still wore the uniform of a colonel of the Corps of Engineers and where from his window at the Pentagon he had a fine view of the yachts on the Potomac River. Around his feet were scattered packing cases stuffed with a career stretching from West Point to the jungles of Nicaragua. His bare room echoed as he moved from case to case filled with graduation pictures and framed diplomas. He paused over a picture of his West Point class, but was distracted by a sudden burst of singing from the corridor. A tortured rendition of 'For He's a Jolly Good Fellow' grew louder and louder. Then, like a finale from a Broadway spectacular, a chorus line of uniforms presented themselves, framed in the doorway, for the most unmusical '. . . and so say all of us!'

The colonel's attention was caught by an object held above the soldiers' heads. They charged into the room and lowered before his dazzled eyes an enormous cake – a replica of the Pentagon, crowned by a row of candles. A young corporal produced a butcher's knife and thrust the handle towards his boss.

'The Japs had better watch out for you, sir. Good

luck.' The fat man, Colonel Leslie R. Groves, grasped the knife and gazed around at the men. Each was adding to the corporal's message his own rehearsed farewell, but Groves heard nothing they said. He looked again at Corporal Bronson and felt the depth of sincerity in the man's words.

'Thank you, Bronson.'

He glanced down at the cake. 'Well, since I'm the guy who built this place, I oughta be able to eat it.' He dragged the blade straight through the cake, slicing it into two awkward slabs.

The fat man in the elevator gazed sullenly at the ageing concrete as it passed slowly before his eyes. He glanced again at his watch and sighed.

Back at the Pentagon he had endured a long and eventually pointless argument with his superior, General Brehon Somervell. He could recall the office and the way the general had turned every excuse Groves could think of and dumped them into the garbage.

'General, I've sat behind a desk for twenty-four years. I've dug holes for the army all over the world. I built the place we're standing in – and this is what you're giving me . . . this – this *boondoggle*?'

Somervell laid his hand on a stack of files in the centre of his desk. 'If you took the trouble to look into this . . .'

'General, I'm one of the oldest colonels in the US Army, and in a couple of weeks our guys are going to be hitting the beaches. I want to be in the *real* war. This is my last chance. I'm forty-six years old and I want to see combat.'

Somervell just shook his head. 'The Secretary of War wants *you* . . .' and he emphasized his point with a stab of his finger. 'And now hear this, you!' He slid the file material to one side and leaned across the desk.

'This project has been ambling along for two or three years. There's a group of scientists up at the University of Chicago and in a couple of other places around the country gathered together under some vague semi-governmental umbrella, coming up with zilch. The short version is that a bunch of brainboxes are sitting around tossing theories at each other when we need to be manufacturing devices. The damned thing needs to be run properly. It needs army know-how, army organization and god-damned army discipline.'

But Groves was not defeated yet. 'General, for the past year I've been responsible for projects that were spending more than $600 million a month. I've heard of this atomic thing. The whole cockamamie idea has a projected budget of just $100 million – all up.'

Somervell ploughed on. 'Get into all this stuff, Dick,' he said, slapping the stack of files. 'Then get among those eggheads. The one to see first is Szilard. Dick, it's all in here.' Somervell rarely addressed his subordinates by their Christian names, except when he needed something. When Groves let anyone use his name he preferred the short version of his middle name, Richard.

Somervell continued on a different tack. 'Of course, you'll be swapping that chicken on your shoulder for a star. If you're gonna ride hard on a bunch of scientists, you'll need rank – Major General.'

They traded a brief smile and then Somervell leaned across his desk. 'Dick, if you do this right, you could win the war.' Though Somervell meant every word, it still sounded patronizing, and it grated on Groves's self-esteem.

'Oh, that thing.'

Somervell swivelled out from behind his desk. It was a signal that the meeting was over. 'You'll get whatever you need. Anything, but one thing. What you haven't got, is time.'

General Groves stood outside Room 1112 and rapped on the door. There was no reply. He knocked again. Nothing. Then he gave the door a series of solid thumps.

'General Groves?' The voice came from inside. The general pushed at the door and it opened.

'General, is that you?'

Inside, the door to the bathroom stood slightly ajar. Groves moved cautiously towards it.

'Come in.'

This kind of civilian indifference annoyed him. 'Professor Szilard?' He pronounced it Sigh-lard.

'Ze-*lard*. Ze-*lard*.'

'Right. Got it.'

Groves opened the door and was immediately embraced by a cloud of steam. When it cleared he was presented with a vision of bohemian decadence. There in the centre of the tiny room, in a bath filled almost to the brim, protruded a pair of feet at one end and a little round head at the other.

'General Groves?' The Hungarian pronounced 'general' with a hard G and it really got under Groves's skin. He leaned against the door-frame, taking it all in. Every so often he allowed himself a slight shake of the head. It was a new world to him, but he knew it was a world he had first to learn about – then master.

'I was expecting you, but I forgot the time. Forgive me. I get in when everyone has gone to work and . . . I get stuck. Metaphorically.'

Groves knew he had to get used to these people. It was just going to be another problem to solve. He stepped inside, closed the door and slipped the bolt. Then he slid a small stool over beside the bath and eased his bulk on to it. He started some form of conventional greeting, but the situation was too ridiculous, so he resorted to his briefcase. He removed the file marked SZILARD, detached the letter to the president and held it before the scientist's bright, bird-like gaze.

'I've read this. And I've read all the other reports from Chicago. Is it possible?' asked Groves.

'You couldn't put a little hot in here, could you . . .?'

Groves locked the paper away again, then he leaned over and turned on the hot tap. 'I think you guys know that I represent your paymaster from here on in. Now, I've got no time for fairy tales, Professor. Let's have the happy ending.'

With dignity, Szilard pulled himself up in the bath, while water slopped dangerously close to the general.

'It's possible. In fact, it's probably inevitable. Separate Uranium 235, then arrange for two portions of the new element to be brought together suddenly, so that the resulting mass – no bigger than a pineapple, General . . .' Again the hard G. '. . . undergoes a spontaneous, self-sustaining reaction. Then, if this was the epicentre of that explosion, everything that you can see of Chicago would disintegrate.'

Groves got up from his stool and crossed to the tiny window at the head of the bath. He slowly wiped away the condensation and revealed the spreading city. As he thought over what the scientist had just told him, Szilard levered himself from the bath, towelled himself off and slipped into the most tasteless black silk Japanese dressing-gown Groves had ever seen. He then gathered up his belongings and stood by the open door. Groves glanced across just in time to see the Hungarian jerk his head towards the bedroom.

Szilard's single room was almost bare of furniture and yet the over-all impression was one of suffocating clutter. A table by the window was covered by stacks of technical papers, files were piled on the chairs and even his bed was littered with last night's scribblings. To Groves, who was meticulous, this was chaos. More than that, it was wilful neglect of the most fundamental principles of security. He lowered himself into the only reasonably clear armchair, while restraining the impulse to bawl Szilard out and then escape from the mess. Meanwhile, the Hungarian had slipped on his spectacles and was pacing back and forth with a sheaf of papers in his hand.

'Now. To answer your question, can we do this. Of course it can be done.'

'But you all seem to be bogged down at the moment,' countered Groves.

'At the moment we have theories, concepts, inspirations, a few inconclusive results. We are trying to calculate the amount of fissionable material we will need to make a bomb – and we've made good progress. In fact, we have a figure now, correct to a factor of ten,' he said proudly.

'A factor of ten! What can I do with figures like that? How can I construct a factory to produce these devices when we don't know whether we're building three bombs, thirty bombs or three-tenths of a bomb?'

Szilard shrugged. To him Groves's anxiety seemed an irrelevance. The general went on to the attack again. 'Just exactly how much of this . . . this fission stuff do we have?'

'Uranium 235?' Szilard added.

'Right. How much is there in the country?'

'Well. They're producing the stuff out at Berkeley. My understanding is that they have no sizeable quantities yet.'

'None?' asked Groves.

'A few milligrams, 30 per cent pure.' Groves's fist came down in despair on to the arm of his chair. Szilard took what he saw to be an opportunity to make up some ground. 'It's clear we need some proper organization, coordination – a vision.' He meant his own. 'You'll need a physicist to lead the team of scientists, and of course you'll need money. This will be expensive.'

Groves was suspicious of people who presumed to lecture him about organization. As his eyes roamed across the muddle about him he knew 'these self-appointed authorities on everything' couldn't organize a tea party. Yet he agreed with one point: the technicalities of the project were way beyond him. He would need a project leader, a scientist – but not this one.

'If we can build this device, so can others,' Groves pronounced.

'Exactly.' At last, Szilard thought, some common ground. 'Germany has good, capable scientists. They have the necessary industrial base and, in Czechoslovakia, they have access to the raw material. So . . .'

'So what do we need, Professor?' asked Groves.

Szilard looked Groves in the eye. 'To beat them to it,' he replied.

TWO

A thin band of concrete wound through the hills east of San Francisco, rising higher and higher towards the San Joaquin Valley. The sun had cleared the brow of the hills and had just begun to warm the soft, rolling countryside. At this time of the morning convoys of military vehicles moved slowly through the traffic towards the city. In the opposite direction a single, bright yellow streak had the highway all to itself and it ate up the road at a terrific speed.

It was an open-top Series 70 Roadmaster Sport Phaeton, a magnificent riot of chrome and power. Behind the wheel a young, strikingly attractive man piloted the metal beast towards the sun. He was J. Robert Oppenheimer, one of the most talented young physicists in the country. Beside him sat his wife Katherine and, hunched up in the narrow back seat, was his brother Frank. As they thundered their way up the hills, Kitty was thrilled by her husband's speed. She loved to see the exhilaration in his face as he felt the power at his disposal, and she enjoyed her growing sense of terror. She threw a glance across her shoulder, and exploded with laughter. Frank clutched the back of his brother's seat and looked seriously ill. Every time Robert changed gears and revved the engine, Frank's head tossed back into the wind and his grip on the seat tightened.

Just past the little town of Livermore Oppenheimer brought the machine down to a throaty roar and steered it on to a narrow, partly sealed road, straight past an official 'No Entry' sign. Despite the rough road, Oppenheimer had absolute faith in his suspension.

'So tell us about this general,' said Kitty inquiringly.

'Why?'

'Because it's all so mysterious. You're invited to a meeting in the middle of God knows where. You're supposed to be there not before 4.20 and not later than 4.29.' She looked over at Frank to share her incredulity, but his attention was somewhere down at his feet. She glanced back at Robert and nudged him for a response.

'Well, all I've heard is that he's an overweight windbag who has spent his life digging holes for the US army in Latin America.'

'Graves for the natives, no doubt,' Frank muttered from the back seat.

'Oh, come on, Frank. You hate anyone in uniform. The streets are filled with uniforms these days – you can't hate them all.'

'When the military start approaching scientists, I get suspicious. Once you get sucked in, they'll take all of you. You'll turn into one of them.'

'All of me, why not take all of me . . .' Kitty sang. Oppenheimer laughed at the thought of the military transforming him into one of their automatons.

'Come on, Frank. *Ohne Wissen, Ohne Sünde*,' which meant 'Without knowledge, without sin.' 'All I'm doing is going to talk with the man and see what he has to offer. I'm not joining the army.' Oppenheimer pressed down on the accelerator.

'Jesus, Robert. Do we need to go this fast?'

'Yes!'

'It's beautiful,' screamed Kitty.

'Yes, it's beautiful!'

'It's crazy!' said Frank, looking down at the floor of the car again.

With that remark still hanging in the air the whole scene was suddenly tipped to the brink of tragedy. A jack-rabbit, slicing invisibly through the brushwood, suddenly froze in the middle of the road. Oppenheimer saw it, instantly hit the brakes and swerved across to the left. The rear of the car swung round, the vehicle slid sideways towards the far side of the road and scraped across the gravel. Kitty was thrown into the windscreen while Frank was almost catapulted out altogether. Once it had all stopped, the car – magically – was still upright.

'You OK?' Robert asked as he collected Kitty in his arms. Kitty allowed herself to be held and nodded, somewhat breathless. The gravel and dust settled and all that could be heard was the innocent tick-over of the engine. Frank now leaped out of the back and strode around the vehicle. He was almost speechless. He looked at the couple holding each other in the front of the car and he almost burst with rage.

'Why didn't you just hit it?'

The couple untied themselves and Oppenheimer crunched the gears into reverse.

'Robert?'

Frank had always felt dominated by his brother. Robert steered the car back to the right side of the road and found first gear. Frank followed. He always felt as though Robert would leave him behind.

'I mean, why . . .?' he said as he got back into the car.

Oppenheimer considered the question. 'Because it was alive,' he said at last.

'You nearly killed us!'

'No, I didn't.' He glanced at his watch. It was 4.10 and their destination was still five miles down the road.

Captain Peer de Silva glanced at his watch. It was now past 4.20 and there was no sign of Oppenheimer. He stood in an empty, open-windowed control tower that overlooked the airfield. Dressed in a civilian suit, there was no indication that he or his colleague beside him had anything to do with the military, but de Silva was in charge of security for Los Alamos. It was his job to check out the credentials of anyone the general wanted to know about. He had already run up a file on the man they called 'Oppie', and he didn't care for what he'd uncovered at all.

'What's he like?' asked his colleague.

'Teaches over at Berkeley. Fuckin' prima donna. Doesn't read newspapers, loves gourmet cooking, fancy wines and fast cars.'

With that de Silva pulled a pair of binoculars up to his face and scanned a faint smear of dust on the horizon.

'Jesus! Fuckin' prima donna's gone and brought a

picnic!' He concentrated hard on the distant target. 'OK. Oppenheimer's at the wheel, wife in the passenger seat. In back is brother Frank. He was the Communist. Left the Party in 1940, apparently.'

De Silva started down the wooden staircase and his colleague followed.

'Now, here's how it goes. The family stays at the gatehouse, got it?'

'Right.'

'Send Oppenheimer over this way.'

Corporal Bronson and Oppenheimer marched together across the runway towards the vast black void before them, heading towards an aircraft hangar that loomed like a fortress on an otherwise barren plain, through doors so big you could drag a cathedral through them.

'Sorry about all that,' said Bronson. 'The general sees you on your own.'

Oppenheimer walked silently beside him and didn't bother to respond. As they entered the vast space, their footsteps echoed up and down the walls. Moving from the glare of the concrete into the gloom of Valhalla, Oppenheimer was momentarily blinded. On either side he could almost make out the shape of a wing or the looming face of an aircraft engine. There was no accident involved in this arrangement. The parade past these machines of war might have seemed ludicrously theatrical, if perhaps it hadn't been so sinister.

'Wait here,' said Bronson. Oppenheimer drew a deep breath and filled his lungs with the scent of aircraft fuel and oil.

'Good morning, Doctor. Come on up.'

Oppenheimer turned towards the voice and found himself in front of the overwhelming mass of an aircraft. The B24, the 'Liberator'. Spread out before him, in either direction, seemed to be an endless display of bright, shiny aluminium.

He moved cautiously forward and found himself at the foot of steps that led up to the main crew entrance. There, towering above him, was the equally huge shape of Leslie R. Groves.

'General Groves?'

'Come and take a look.' Groves disappeared into the body of the beast while Oppenheimer was still mounting the steps. Inside he found a maze of delicately laced wires and cables concentrated into a single functioning device of calculated mass destruction. The young man trod warily towards the cockpit where Groves was squeezing himself into the pilot's seat. Oppenheimer stood behind him, uncertain whether to proceed any deeper into the beast. Groves flashed him a quick look and then gestured at the array of controls.

'Ingenuity. I love it. Everything has a single purpose, fits just right into its place and does its job. And all of it created right outa here,' he smiled, tapping his temple. The smile surprised the scientist, until he looked at the eyes above the smile: those were as welcoming as the Arctic. The next move really took Oppenheimer by surprise. Groves slipped his hand across to a panel of switches and tipped one of them to ignition. From outside the glass canopy came a steady whine, which grew louder and louder.

'Don't worry, we ain't gonna fly, Doctor. We're just gonna talk.' The engine suddenly exploded into life and the most tremendous roar filled the hangar with a sound like fire and brimstone. Groves gently pushed forward on the throttle, lifting the revs just above idle. He checked the brake compression and was satisfied. He sat there for a moment, feeling the power tremble through the aircraft, then he leaned forward, slid a panel of plexi-glass into place and the cockpit was suddenly quiet.

'Come on.' Groves heaved himself out of the seat and headed towards the rear of the plane. In the section that would normally have been the bomb bay, a false floor had been added and rows of seating laid on top. Groves collapsed into one seat and Oppenheimer followed the general's example and took the seat opposite. Here they were, face to face.

There could not have been two more different people. General Groves, working as a field-hand by the age of eleven, had been brought up, the son of a clergyman, in a simple yet puritanical rural home and had struggled through military academies to get to West Point. He often declared that he had studied for a full ten years after entering college: 'That would be the equivalent of about two Ph.D.s, wouldn't it,' he liked to joke. He had a reputation as someone who could get things done. He was a mover of mountains. He seemed to get what he wanted by bullying and desk-thumping, yet those who knew him best, and his superiors, who had great admiration for him, even if they didn't always like him, knew that behind the bully-boy exterior lay a razor-sharp mind, a mind that, computer-like, would calculate the odds, assess the possibilities, and reach a decision, all in a few lightning seconds.

His great talent then lay in making others think they had written the music, when all along they were marching to Groves's tune. His weakness – especially in an environment like the army – was that he was easily shocked by references to sex. He didn't swear, was a teetotaller and his only vice was an absolutely insatiable appetite for chocolate.

Across the way sat the 'boy wonder'. The child of wealthy Jewish parents, Robert had grown up in a large apartment on New York's Riverside Drive. At the age Groves was earning pennies sweating in a field, Oppenheimer had delivered a scientific paper to the New York Mineralogical Club. At eighteen he had his own 28-foot sloop which he used to take up and down the coast of Long Island. He studied at the Cavendish Institute in England and the Leyden Institute in Germany. He spoke fluent French and German, he knew ancient Greek and Latin and he had taught himself Sanskrit.

Groves was a towering figure, a non-smoking puritan. Oppenheimer was a frail, hedonistic five-pack-a-day man who despised fat people.

Outside, the hangar reverberated with the sound of thirty-two cylinders roaring away. Bronson heaved against a heavy soundproofed door at the far end of the building and entered a little sanctuary occupied by de Silva and his friend in the overcoat. Bronson stood for a moment, rubbing his ears.

'The egghead wants a carrot juice.'

'Jesus,' laughed the overcoat.

'Get him what he wants, Bronson. And get used to it,' muttered de Silva.

*

Back in the Liberator Groves had already gone through all the sensitive material. Without warning, he heaved himself towards the cockpit and cut the engine. The massive machine slowly stopped its trembling and settled back into silence. Groves stopped at the door from the cockpit and examined the back of Oppenheimer's head. The young man was deep in thought, thoughts that had all been carefully planted by the general. Groves swung himself back into the seat opposite Oppenheimer and paused for a moment. Then he took hold of the man's gaze with a look that went straight through him.

'I have one further piece of news for you: I want you to run the project.'

'Me?'

'I think you're the man to do it . . . and I have a fatal weakness for good men.'

Oppenheimer said nothing.

'They tell me you have one of the best minds in the country,' added Groves.

'They're right,' the scientist replied. Groves settled back in his seat and waited for the young man to move on. Oppenheimer said, 'I just wonder if you've taken into consideration all the possible consequences of a project like this.'

'That's the real issue, Doctor – the consequences if we don't move now. The Germans are waging a technological war in Europe. They've got aircraft and tanks that are years ahead of anything we've produced. We know they have an atomic project, and they've been at it for years. Do you imagine Hitler would hesitate for one second if he had one of those things?'

'Are you sure about the German project?'

'Ask Szilard. Ask Fermi, or even your boss Laurence out at Berkeley.'

A brief silence fell between them while Groves let these details sink in. Then he took up his theme again. 'Tell me something. Where would you start? What would your priorities be?'

Oppenheimer was at home with hypotheses: 'Focus. There's a lot of talent out there, some truly great minds, but they're all dancing to a different tune. Bring them together in one place. Isolated. No distractions. Create a climate of stress – creative stress. Everyone competing for the same answer – then you'll get your solution. All you'll need is a ringmaster.'

'All right!' Groves could tell that the boy had already said yes.

'You've got Szilard and Laurence pulling one way, Conant and the Chicago group another, Compton at Columbia in yet another. It's fragmented and all over the place. Centralize.'

'Great. Now, I'm going to level with you. There's a lot of opposition to your being considered for this job. Your political background stinks, you know that?'

The news unsettled Oppenheimer only slightly. '*Mens curiosa non est semper secura* – A curious mind is not always safe.'

'Well, it had better be. You could win the war *and* a Nobel Prize with this project, Doctor . . . God willing.' Then, leaning closer to the scientist, Groves lowered his voice. 'Do you know why I want you for this job?'

'No. Tell me.'

'I read something you wrote about solving problems. You said, "Eliminate the elements you don't need, refine the question and commit to the answer."

I like that. Eliminate, refine, commit. You're no shrinking violet, Doctor. This is the biggest, most important scientific project of the century. And it's yours.'

Suddenly Corporal Bronson staggered into the cabin. 'Pardon me, General. Captain de Silva said to remind you that you've got a train to catch at 1800 hours.'

'Well, no rest for the wicked,' laughed Groves as he lifted himself out of his seat. He laid a hand on Oppenheimer's thin shoulder. 'Just one more thing, Doctor. And I say this in all humility, because no one respects genius more than I do. If you accept, you'll be answerable to me. Sleep on it.'

THREE

At the Oppenheimer house in Berkeley the lights went out late that night. As the rambling wooden structure settled in the cool air, Robert and Kitty lay together listening to the night – distanced by their separate thoughts. They heard the sycamore brushing against the house. Kitty caressed his long, delicate hand, while Robert stared at the lights streaking across the ceiling. There before him was the face of the fat man, and his words echoed still.

'Will you take it?' Kitty asked quietly.

'Well, there are still questions, all sorts of questions. And if it ever came to actually . . . Anyway, they've already started work.'

'If you'd rather wait, I don't really need to know.'

'You should. You'll be wife to the big cheese.'

Suddenly interested, Kitty lifted herself on to her elbows. 'Does it mean moving? Will it be an interesting crowd?' She peered into his face but there wasn't the slightest sign for her. She was shut out again. 'I think you should take it.'

'You don't know what it is yet.'

'Doesn't matter. You're too brilliant for this place.' She rolled against him, brushing her breasts against his arm. 'They'll bury you here, and you'll be forgotten.'

He turned and looked at her properly.

'Say yes, Robert. You deserve more than this.' He slid his arm under her shoulders and drew her to him. 'We deserve more than this.' She smiled.

They kissed and were about to move on to other things when they were distracted by a noise from the corridor.

'Mom, I want a drink of water.'

Kitty buried her face in Robert's chest. 'Well, you know where it is.'

Robert uncurled his arm and returned to the images on the ceiling.

'Mom?'

'Just a minute.' Kitty peeled herself away from Robert's warmth and sat up on the edge of the bed. 'Come on, Peter, back to bed. I'll be there in a minute.' She turned back. 'Robert.'

'Yeah?'

'I've been thinking – about another baby. I need to know if you're going to accept.'

'*A bon chien, il ne va jamais un bon os . . .*'

'Does that mean yes?'

'See, one small word and . . .' She tumbled back into his warmth, ready to explode with joy. She nuzzled her face against his cheek, but he was already gone, his eyes tossing bright beads of light before him. There was nothing to share.

'Mom?' the little one complained. Kitty twisted off the bed and put an arm around her son's shoulders. At the door she glanced back at the figure stretched along the bed.

'Will it change everything?' she asked.

'Everything,' he said, mouthing each syllable separately.

At the physics department of the University of California at Berkeley, J. Robert Oppenheimer's classes were famous. He held an audience of young minds in thrall as he eloquently explored the secrets of the universe. His classes were not filled only with diagrams explaining particle physics, but also with paintings and drawings describing the vast embrace of the universal human experience. He would read Plato aloud in the original Greek, quote Catullus in Latin and discuss the philosophy of predestination. It was not uncommon for students to ask to take his course over again, just to prolong the experience. And at the end of that autumn semester, as he brought his work to a close, they were there again, filling the lecture theatre. There wasn't even standing room at the back.

Oppenheimer stood to the side of a screen on to which was projected the semi-naked Renaissance figures that heralded the creation.

'So there, in balance, *carissime fratelli,* origin and destiny: sensuously expressed in Michelangelo's ceiling of the Sistine Chapel – and revealed also, little by little, as we cast light upon the awesome and sometimes beautiful landscape of physics. Origin and destiny. Think about it.' With those words still running through the students' minds, he stepped down from the platform and moved to the softly humming epidiascope. 'So. To repolish a phrase from Rilke: *So leben wir, und nehmenn immer Abscheid.*' And with that he doused the image.

He looked to his audience for the translation. It was a familiar test, and an uneven chorus replied: 'Thus we live, forever taking leave.'

He smiled and turned back for his papers. 'You know, of course, that this is the last class I shall give you good people. It's also my last class here at Berkeley.' The audience delivered up their disappointment with groans and shouts of 'No!', which Oppenheimer took with a semi-serious bow. 'And as I leave to discover my own small destiny . . .' With the smallest gesture of his hand, he elicited absolute quiet and his mood became serious. '. . . I just want to congratulate all of you for being – really – the best, the very best of the best. I thank you all. I have faith in you all and God keep you all. May your days be rich and sweet.'

The audience leaped to their feet and the applause resounded up and down the corridors. As he stood before them, apparently drinking in their gratitude, his eyes slowly scanned their faces. Then he caught sight of her. Dark and beautiful, much older than most of his students, though still quite young. Her gaze had been fixed on him throughout and she beamed when their eyes met. She read his silent signal and moved slowly towards the exit. Oppenheimer had missed the character in the raincoat, standing towards the back of the room. He, on the other hand, hadn't missed Oppenheimer's signal, and when the woman left he followed.

He had parked his car in a leafy suburban street off Solano Avenue, away from the campus. Beside him sat Jean Tatlock, a blush of excitement on her face. 'I shouldn't be doing this. I'm a married man.'

'I was there first . . .'

'Ah, but you gave me up, remember?'

A nervous smile flickered across her mouth and she found it hard to look him in the eye. 'I know . . . I – I'm sorry but I needed to see you now. I need to feel close to you. Not constantly, but sometimes.'

Robert threw his arm around her and they buried themselves in a long, deep kiss. They touched each other, kissing each other hard again and again. It had been too long.

They didn't notice the dark Chevrolet rolling quietly in neutral to a spot some twenty yards behind them. In the Chevy, de Silva and his buddy in the raincoat were taking pictures, wishing they could hear what they were talking about in Oppenheimer's car.

'I'm going to be away from Berkeley for a while. I've been offered something,' said Robert.

Jean and Robert had met in 1936, when she was working for her doctorate in psychology. The daughter of a history professor at Berkeley, Jean had become a member of the Communist Party the year before that. As their love affair developed, she claimed she had awakened his social conscience, and had encouraged him to spend some of his wealth on the Party's campaigns. He had also spent lavishly on jewellery and other expensive gifts for her. But their relationship had been tortured. They had come to the brink of marriage on two occasions and on both Jean had backed away from the commitment. Most of the problems lay with Jean's emotional state. A manic-depressive, she would swing from the darkest of moods to bizarre, vitriolic attacks on Robert, making him listen to stories of her relationships with other men. She had repeatedly undergone psychiatric treatment and, after yet another period of black despair, had broken off the relationship for good. That was in 1939. Since then, of course, for Robert there had been Kitty.

De Silva was not much interested in Oppenheimer's extra-curricular activities in general. It was not the 'what', it was the 'who' that worried him. Jean was an extremely influential figure on the Berkeley campus. Although he knew her membership of the Communist Party of America was based on idealism, he also knew that many of her colleagues held commitments that ran far deeper than wanting a fair and just society for all. And Jean, like many romantic Communists, held in deep suspicion anything to do with the government, and had a horror of the military.

'I can't stay out of it. As a Jew, as an American, as a human being . . . What do you want me to do, pretend the Nazis don't exist?'

'No, but . . .'

'I've been asked to do something extraordinary. Working with some of the most original minds in the world. I can't just pass it up.'

He brushed his fingers across her cheek. 'In a way, it's what I've been waiting for, a project of real scientific importance. And I'm doing it entirely on my terms, believe me.'

She leaned back against the door and gazed across at the anonymous houses, at their innocent little gardens, at the Chevrolet parked at the end of the street.

'Jean, you were the one who taught me that life had to be lived outside the lab.'

'Every strange extraordinary scrap of it. But life is not full of good faith and promises – and Washington is full of wolves.'

'I'm not going to Washington. The whole thing is wrapped around this general, a real meatball. He'll be nibbling out of the palm of my hand within a week.'

Jean allowed a tiny laugh and a shake of her head. Poor Robert, she thought, staring ahead. She turned to say something, then changed her mind.

'Yes?'

'Nothing. I was going to say something awful about radical professors and domesticity.' She looked hard into his eyes. 'I want you to take this thing on, but please be careful. And don't leave me in the dark. I won't ask for much, just that if I need to see you, you know – that we stay in touch . . .'

The train thundered through the Midwestern night, carving its way across the wheatfields near Wichita, towards what was then the little village of Las Vegas, and then on to Santa Fe, New Mexico. The journey seemed filled with urgency and purpose as the train cut across level-crossings and pierced the heart of the countryside. Inside, the sense of purpose was much less apparent. In the corridors, choked with men in khaki and with their luggage, the atmosphere was heavy with cigarette smoke, stultifying boredom and exhaustion. Through the midst of all this, a young man in a leather flying-jacket, a railway ticket between his teeth, forced his way past the mass of unyielding bodies. At the window of each compartment, he paused to check inside, before continuing the struggle.

Finally, his face pressed hard against the glass immediately beneath a large red sign that said RESERVED, he saw a vision of empty seats. He slid the door to one side, caught sight of a large man in a heavy suit at the end of the compartment and tossed him a wink. General Groves, in civilian clothes, watched impassively as the youngster heaved his suitcase and kit-bag up on to the rack above.

'Didn't you ever go to school?'

'Sure.'

'Didn't they teach you to read, then?' The young man finally gave the general his attention, but was not easily intimidated. In a mock-sympathetic voice, he replied, 'Sure did.'

Groves leaned towards him and stabbed his finger at the sign on the door. 'That, young man, says reserved.'

'Right.' He got to his feet, but only to remove the flying-jacket and reveal the uniform of a captain underneath. 'Listen, buster, I'm authorized to take this compartment. Truth be told here, I myself am on a secret mission.' Richard Shoenfield was a medical radiologist, one of hundreds of specialists that had been summoned from their quiet institutional backgrounds and sent deep into the empty foothills of the Rocky Mountains. Shoenfield was young, terribly self-confident and had what he felt was a healthy contempt for authority.

The general watched this freshly made captain feel about in the bottom of an over-full briefcase, and knew instantly that he was another of those goddam eggheads. Out of the briefcase tumbled a sheaf of papers, and with them a buff-coloured official-looking envelope. Groves sighed under his breath as he stooped to collect it off the floor and hand it back.

'Thanks. Stick of gum?'

'No thanks.'

Shoenfield knew he was out of line, but the uniform had given him a false sense of importance. Besides, the guy opposite seemed in no hurry to do anything, so he figured he'd enjoy the situation a little.

'In fact, I shouldn't even be talking to you. I mean, you look like a regular guy – but, the minute my back is turned you might be making contact with some Nazi spy or something. Know what I mean?'

Groves had been staring straight ahead, but now he turned the full weight of his gaze on the upstart.

'I can tell you this, though: it's submarine work.'

'You in the navy?'

Shoenfield couldn't believe the guy. He jerked his thumb at his uniform. 'Jeez . . . See this colour? Khaki – the U S Army, lowest of the low.'

Groves gave nothing away.

'Look, the Germans have got these land-submarines. Pretty soon they'll be boring all across this country – like moles.' But Shoenfield's story was interrupted as the door slid open and three senior officers stepped into the compartment. They froze at the sight of the captain and then checked the situation out with Groves.

'Everything all right, General?'

Shoenfield took in the gold clasps and scrambled eggs – two colonels and a lieutenant-colonel. Groves nodded calmly and Shoenfield took his cue to exit fast. He hauled his baggage down from the rack and edged towards the door. 'It's been a pleasure, gentlemen.' But he hadn't quite got through the doorway when the fat man shot him a remark.

'Captain!' Shoenfield turned to collect his punishment. 'God, in all his wisdom, graced your face with five holes. Two to look through, two to breathe through and one, if you'll take my advice, you'll concentrate on keeping tightly shut!' Shoenfield backed out into the corridor and was quickly swamped in the sea of khaki.

Once the door was shut Groves beckoned to one of the colonels to come and sit by him. Boris T. Pash was an army Intelligence officer with a passion for undercover work. He was one of a number of people who had the gravest suspicions about Robert Oppenheimer. In fact, Pash and de Silva were both convinced that the general's lead scientist was a Communist spy.

Sitting opposite the general was Lieutenant-Colonel Latrobe, recently assigned to the team. Groves wasn't concerned with security at this time, though. He had much more fundamental priorities.

'They ought to put a bell round that dummy. Latrobe, what's the latest from Oak Ridge?'

'The site has been delivered. The contractor moves in tomorrow.'

'Great. And Hanford?'

'Workers. We need 60,000 and so far we've recruited about 25,000.'

'Well, rustle them up. Give them double rations. Gasolene, booze, whatever it takes.'

'Right.'

'OK, Boris? We need some hard information on Germany – real bad.'

'That's something we just don't have.'

'Boris, simple priorities. How far ahead are they? Where are their key installations? Who are their top people?'

'I get the picture.' Pash took a quick survey of the faces before him before he launched into his speech. 'All we know for certain is that we're still playing catch-up. We're putting together plans for a top-secret, sort of – investigative team. After the landing in France, we want these guys to advance with the front-line troops to search out German installations. We call it ALSOS. In the meantime, we've had some intelligence through British sources that there's something in the Black Forest region, near a town called Bisengen.'

'When does all this happen?'

'If you listen to Churchill, sometime next year. But our guys are saying spring of '44 – at the earliest.'

'No good. I need the info *now*.'

FOUR

About thirty miles north-west of Santa Fe, in the heart of New Mexico, there once stood the Los Alamos Riding School, a small complex of log cabins surrounding the exclusive Fuller Lodge, where the wealthy could send their children for some traditional western toughening-up. Since the outbreak of the war, the riding school had been going through hard times, and the owners were delighted, in November 1942, when the U S Government offered to buy them out. There, amongst the rolling, pine-covered foothills of the Rockies, Groves and Oppenheimer set up their main laboratory – the nerve centre of the Manhattan Project. They had set out on the greatest top-secret project in military history: to build the world's first atomic bomb.

Construction crews arrived almost immediately to begin on the new township. The site lay just above the snow-line and looked out across gently rolling cattle country. The views were magnificent. In one direction, the Sangre de Cristo range nestled in a constant purple haze, in another the Jemez Mountains stood on their own giant green mesa, a long extinct volcano. This breathtaking setting had quickly been invaded by convoys of bulldozers, trucks with lumber from Canada and hundreds of grinding cement-mixers. The canyon soon echoed to the sound of hammers as a bustling, pre-fabricated township sprang up; roads were laid, water found and pumped, electricity laid on and, most importantly, the people began to move in.

Oppenheimer had scoured virtually every university and institute in the country for specialists in the necessary fields. The first year it was like being at a primitive summer camp for the intellectually elite. Professors rubbed shoulders with hard-nosed army engineers and, in the midst of all the chaos, Groves's presence was felt everywhere, urging people on.

The general had arrived in a standard army Buick for one of his regular progress inspections just after a heavy mountain rainstorm. Vehicles were bogged down to their axles and men in mud-stained khaki were manoeuvring bulldozers, dragging the mud for stranded cars. With Groves were Colonels Latrobe and Pash, who stepped out of the Buick only to find themselves marooned in a sea of mud. But Groves, on the other hand, was at home among the filth of a construction site. He headed straight for the site manager, Jack Carter.

'Give me some good news, Jack.'

'Well, we've got utilities throughout the camp, and we've got the sewage now. We have water down throughout and the two labs are pretty much finished, sir. We've got four of the technical buildings completed, another four at the foundation stage. If it hadn't been for the goddam rain . . .'

'That's not good enough. We must be a couple of

weeks behind.' Groves jerked his thumb in the direction of Santa Fe. 'Look, I've got a bunch of eggheads up there wandering around, bumping into each other. They need roofs over their heads. I want to see more construction workers up here in a week. The next time I'm through here, I want to hear you're ahead of schedule.'

'General, I don't think there's accommodation for any more . . .' interrupted Latrobe.

'What do they need accommodation for? You think they're gonna sleep, Latrobe? Get a bunch of tents for them, if that'll help your conscience.'

Above their heads, pre-fab buildings were being jibbed across the chaos to their selected markings. Concrete mixers chugged away on each newly designated block, while pneumatic compressors made conversation almost impossible. Groves strode onwards through it all, punctuating his words with violent gestures.

'Latrobe, I asked for dogs on the perimeter fences. Where are they?'

'They're coming, General.'

The heart of the new township would be the old Fuller Lodge, which was to become a kind of restaurant-cum-community centre. Oppenheimer's house, and those of the other key scientists, were the old log cabins that had previously been used by the riding-school instructors. They were situated on 'Bathtub Row', named thus because these were the only buildings with baths in the bathrooms. All other accommodation was fitted with showers and consequently an address on Bathtub Row placed you at the top of the scale. Food and provisions were transported alongside bricks and mortar. Fresh vegetables, the best quality meat – all at roadside-diner prices. The food was a small compensation for having to live in the heart of a construction site.

Most of the wives settled in with a spirit of adventure and acted with a kind of frontier *esprit de corps*. Kitty was the exception. Official entertaining bored her, but the impromptu gathering became her forte, especially if it involved plenty of drink. Most of the other wives found her a somewhat daunting character. Brash and frankly spoken, her conversation was often sprinkled with expletives that other women only expected to hear on the construction site.

Kitty was a bundle of contradictions. She'd been born in Germany and was related to German aristocracy. In fact, her cousin was Hitler's Army Chief of Staff, a fact she enjoyed revealing to her confidants. Though she'd been brought up in America and her accent betrayed no hint of her origins, she nevertheless ran her home with Teutonic thoroughness and was obsessed with her social status amongst the other wives at Los Alamos. Despite this, she seemed shockingly vulgar to them. Sitting on the floor with a drinking companion, a bottle of whisky between them, Kitty confessed that she had been married three times before and had allowed herself to get pregnant so that Robert would marry her. They had nicknamed Peter 'Pronto' when he was born six months later. 'She was a bitch, but an elegant bitch,' Franz Goethe's wife remarked.

Robert largely ignored his wife's social foibles at Los Alamos. He was completely overwhelmed by the speed with which everything had happened. The new environment made the job doubly stimulating. He had ridden these hills many times as a young man and had chosen the site because he loved the surrounding countryside. Living in a log cabin high up in the mountains surrounded by the best minds in the country gave him a real charge.

As Groves made his inspection, Robert and his son Peter were playing at trying to set the lunch table. Kitty watched from the kitchen as the large white tablecloth was shaken high into the air. As it floated to the ground like a parachute, Robert ducked underneath and transformed himself into a ghostly bogeyman. This sent Kitty into convulsions, while the toddler was torn between horror and delight. It was a rare scene of domestic bliss. Robert had never had much contact with his son and almost never played with him. The domestic area of his life he left to Kitty or the maid. Here was a transformation. Then, just as the bogeyman made as if to leap across the table, the doorbell rang.

The bogeyman opened the door and then ushered the general into the living room, folding the tablecloth over his arm.

'We were just laying the table.'

Groves nodded politely. He smiled awkwardly at the little chap standing before him, but had no words to add.

'Lunch is almost ready,' Kitty called from the kitchen.

'Oh, well . . .'

Oppenheimer checked his watch. 'I didn't realize it was so late. We've got a general meeting at two.'

Kitty emerged from the kitchen. 'No time for lunch?'

She was just in time to see Groves pushing Oppenheimer towards the door. 'I am sorry, but we'll be late. The gong rings for everybody, Oppie, I'm afraid.'

Kitty watched the pair of them moving through the chaos and felt the first sharp sting of resentment – the presence of a serious rival. It felt like jealousy.

By that spring of 1943 Groves and Oppenheimer had assembled the most elite assortment of Nobel Prize-winners, professors and young geniuses that had yet been seen in one place. On the day of the interrupted lunch, they had all been summoned to Technical Building A to hear an address from the two project leaders. Groves and Oppenheimer sat at a table at the head of the room in front of nearly fifty of the most inquisitive minds in the country. The average age was about twenty-six. One man who was not present at Los Alamos was Dr Leo Szilard.

For Groves it was one of the brightest moments in his career, and one he savoured long after. He decided not to lecture everyone from the table, but instead he took a chair down towards the front row, turned it backwards and straddled it like a saddle. This would be what the army called a regular bull session.

'Now, I have to talk to you about secrecy.' The word excited a ripple of disapproval. 'What you are going to hear today is not – I repeat *not* – your property. It is the property of the United States Government, to be divulged to no one, however close.' Suddenly everyone was on the edges of their seats.

'So, whatever goes on around here is privileged

information. No exceptions, no wives, no barbers, *no* exceptions. What you read, see, think, hear, dream about, whatever gives you heartburn, keeps you awake at night and feeds your ulcers belongs to me or the US Army, whichever makes you feel more comfortable. We are out of the clouds, gentlemen, and in the business of winning a war.'

He paused to allow the full weight of his words to sink in.

'Now, I will say this once, and only once. Those of you who know it, know it. For those who don't, you're not here to be comfortable. You are here to take yourselves beyond the realm of the theoretical, the speculative or the fanciful and you are here to harness your God-given talents, your minds and your energies, to the practical pursuit of one thing:' again he scanned their faces before continuing – 'a military weapon, a nuclear weapon – an atomic bomb.'

The audience was electrified. Glances shot across from one to another. Some had guessed it, but for others it was a complete shock.

'Keep the muttering down to a minimum, gentlemen. Gentlemen?' And he had silence again. 'Gentlemen, from now on, when you think about it, talk about it, write about it, you will refer to it simply as the "device" or the "gadget". Is that clear?'

As Groves boomed on about cooperation and secrecy, down among the audience one of Szilard's countrymen, Edward Teller, leaned towards his neighbour's ear.

'Why do we bother with a bomb? Why not just drop the general on Berlin? It would have much the same effect.'

*

As the meeting of project leaders continued, chaos still reigned in the streets of this crazy new town. Alongside newly designed scientific equipment, terrifying quantities of high explosives were arriving. In fact, at times there were more explosives on site than in an average military ammunition dump. Picking their way through crates of nitroglycerine, scores of young scientists and engineers tried to make sense of their new lives. One of the newcomers was Michael Merriman, a young physicist who specialized in rare materials. He arrived with a single kit-bag, his favourite baseball bat and utter confusion.

He wandered through the maze of half-built buildings and stacks of equipment, intimidated by the presence of so many military figures. An MP, catching sight of this lost sheep, led him towards a dormitory block across the street.

'When I got to Santa Fe I went to 109 East Palace Street. I was supposed to report to a Mrs McKibben, but there was no one there, so I hitched a ride on a construction bus. I've been sitting on trains and in railway stations and in the backs of buses for the past sixty hours. When I asked them in Santa Fe how to get to this place, they said it didn't exist!'

'It doesn't.' The MP left him at the door to his hut. 'And, if you're planning to take a shower, do it now. The water's all gone by two o'clock.'

Merriman leaned against the door, exhausted, both mentally and physically, and tried the handle. The door wasn't locked, just stuck, but it was the last thing he needed at that moment. In despair he hammered at the door. 'Will someone open this fucking door? Now!'

Suddenly the offending barrier swung open and there, framed in the doorway, was Shoenfield.

'I'm sorry, I couldn't get in . . .'

'A month from now,' said Shoenfield, 'and you'll be hammering to be let out. You Merriman?'

'Yeah.'

'Well, terrific. Richard Shoenfield. Just what we need around here. A roommate bursting with brute strength.'

By now he had been led to the foot of a set of wooden stairs.

'Up, Merriman.' But the way was barred by a massive refrigerator parked halfway up the stairs.

'*What* is that?'

'A refrigerator,' Shoenfield explained patiently.

'Stuck, huh?'

'With a mind like yours . . .'

Merriman dumped his stuff and the two of them clambered up to the machine. Shoenfield climbed over to the far side while Merriman tucked his shoulder into the base. Between them they carried it up to the landing, where they turned it in the opposite direction and wedged it firmly against the banister. It was now stuck once again. Then, as Merriman was about to redouble his efforts, a door on the landing opened and out stepped the most beautiful woman Merriman had ever seen. Clinging to her nurse's uniform, nestled on her shoulder, was a small chimpanzee.

'Ah, Kathleen! Merriman, this is Kathleen Robinson, and Babyface. Babyface is the chimp.' Merriman's eyes echoed his opinion of the nurse.

'Merriman?'

'Michael, actually.'

'Pleased to meet you, Michael.'

The chimp slipped away from her mistress and leaped to Shoenfield's shoulder, where she sat proudly, ruler over all she surveyed.

'She's jealous. Babyface, I mean. And Kathleen, I'm pleased to say, is my fiancée.'

'It's true, Michael. The doctor and I met just after I got here, nearly forty-five minutes ago. We got engaged on the spot. Are you medical like Shoenfield?'

'Honey, no one is like me.' Shoenfield turned in mock despair to Merriman. 'She's so fickle it's embarrassing sometimes.'

Merriman had no attention to give him. 'Not medical, no.' He left it at that. He was completely mesmerized by the woman in front of him.

'Well, Richard, I can't get downstairs with this in the way. And if I'm late for duty, I'll just have to break off our engagement.' The two men returned to the job in hand. As Shoenfield tried to haul the thing towards him, Merriman heaved from beneath. Babyface took the opportunity to leap to the top of the fridge as it rose awkwardly on to the next step. There it hesitated for a moment, wavered and then for no apparent reason lurched to the right, broke through the banister and crashed to the floor below. Babyface squealed with delight and somersaulted in midair.

'See!' declared Shoenfield proudly. 'Oppie's boys! No problem left unsolved.'

At Technical Building A Oppenheimer had taken the floor and was leading his colleagues through his plans.

Groves sat, arms folded, listening to the performance. Oppenheimer had pulled back a set of curtains to reveal a flow-chart that highlighted the various stages of the programme. This deceptively simple diagram was largely made up of four boxes, labelled PHYSICS, FUEL, DEMONSTRATION and DEVICE AVAILABLE.

'We'll be dealing with three main areas: first, the physics. Now, the question we've got to solve straight away, one I know many of you have been working on for a while now, is just how much fissionable material is needed to make the gadget? And equally important – which material? Uranium 235 or plutonium – or both?'

He turned to the flow-chart and slapped his hand against the box marked FUEL. 'Second, manufacture of raw materials. We need to solve the problem of whether U235 can be separated and whether plutonium can be manufactured in sufficient quantities. All that work is going to be carried out at the two new plants that are being built at Oak Ridge in Tennessee and at Hanford, up in Washington state.'

At the mention of these two newly classified locations, Groves felt a brief flush of embarrassment. He shot the professor a disapproving glance, but Oppenheimer was already moving on.

A couple of tentative questions had been asked from the floor.

'Is the place large enough?'

'I have no idea yet.'

'We'll need some test samples. Where will they come from, Mars?'

'Probably. That's not our responsibility. This,' he said, stabbing at the DEMONSTRATION box on the flow-chart, 'this is our responsibility, and it's a cinch!' Nervous laughter scuttled around the room and then died. 'We will build the device, test it and just hope that we'll be able to control it.' He waited until that thought had sunk in and then went back to the beginning of the chart. 'This is where we are now – at the beginning.' Then he moved his finger across the chart to the final box and paused. 'We must get down to here – within nineteen months.'

He looked at his audience, who simply stared back. They were stunned. Many were incredulous, others angry, deciding they had been drafted into a madhouse.

Enrico Fermi's career had already been made. The brilliant Italian was regarded as the foremost physics experimenter in America. He had turned the Pupin Physics Building at Columbia University, where he lectured, into the heartbeat of American nuclear physics. He had already won the Nobel prize and, frankly, he didn't really need to be here.

'Oppie,' he said, in his heavy Italian accent, 'I think I speak for quite a number of us. The project certainly has its attractions. Much of the theoretical work will be, well, challenging, but aren't we being perhaps a little unrealistic about the timeframe? You know there are over a thousand different ways we might approach this situation –'

'Sure I know that, Enrico. That's why I've already decided what route we'll take.' This was almost as startling as the deadline. 'Besides, nineteen months coincides with our anticipated delivery from Oak Ridge. Gentlemen, we have nineteen months to box, wrap and deliver this package. Are you all coming with me?'

The words brought a rush of enthusiasm through the hall. The race was on.

Groves, almost forgotten by the scientists in their enthusiasm, threw Oppie a look of approval. The horse he had put his money on was going to be a front-runner.

FIVE

At Oppenheimer's house the lights blazed across the front yard, which was littered with pieces of construction equipment and the beginnings of a garden. In the kitchen Kitty had battled through the evening with a particularly difficult new stove and with the growing conviction that she was not going to be seeing her husband that night. She hated the kitchen, but the Indian maid was useless. The stove was a simple, if impossible, problem. Once the oven got hot enough for long enough, the door refused to open. It seemed to have developed a will of its own which mirrored her own situation. The hotter it got, the less she could do with it. Deep within the bowels of the little monster supper was being turned into charcoal. Smoke had begun to appear from the back and the oven door had now become too hot to touch.

'What's the matter?' asked Peter from the doorway.

'I've got a pie in here and I can't get it open.' With rising desperation she tugged and wrenched at the handle, until the telephone rang and she surrendered. She tossed the oven gloves to the floor and snatched the phone from the wall.

'Robert, thank God you called.' She took the phone

from her ear and shook it at her son. 'Don't go near it, Peter, it's red hot. Hallo, Robert? Robert – what time will you be home?'

But there was no voice at the other end, just the faint static of a long-distance call. Then the line clicked and died.

'Hallo? Hallo?'

Kitty dropped the receiver back into its cradle and, eyes thoughtful, wary, looked across at the scene in the kitchen. A wave of anxiety flowed through her and she had nothing with which to fight it. She returned to the monster and turned off its power, shepherded her son out of the battle zone, sending him off to his room. In the darkened dining room a row of bottles glinted softly as Kitty closed the door to the kitchen behind her.

The meeting in Technical Building A continued throughout the afternoon and on into the night. They had developed a real head of steam. Minds and collars were open. A couple of blackboards had been pulled out and were now covered with layers of calculations. The rows of chairs had been rearranged into a series of arcs and circles, where separate groups slowly turned the machinery of thought. Jackets had long been discarded, ties loosened and in the air above them a cloud of dense cigarette smoke clung to the lights like mist. At the heart of all the industry, Oppenheimer stood jabbing his finger at each voice from the floor. Groves, though not one of the brotherhood, watched from the sidelines and carefully steered the discussion back when the men got too far away from the main subject, in their enthusiasm for such a beautiful abstract problem. He tugged at a handful of the ever-present chocolate and barked between mouthfuls: 'Give me the problem.'

'Well, it's a question of method,' Robert Serber stammered quietly. Dr Serber had been one of Oppenheimer's students at Berkeley and later his teaching assistant. He was to become one of the team's great diplomats, always knowing just how to deal with all the complex personalities, not least of which was the general. 'Now, the one we have the most faith in is the one we call the gun method. Imagine that it's like firing a shell of one sub-critical mass down the barrel of a cannon. At the top of the barrel we have welded a thick plug of another sub-critical mass. Let me show you.' Serber motioned to the blackboard, but found his way barred by someone standing right in front of it.

Freshly showered and changed, Michael Merriman had only just entered the sanctum and he immediately began to copy the calculations on the board. Serber touched the young stranger on the shoulder and ushered him to one side.

'Now, once we have these two elements in collision with each other, we quickly get a substantial emission of neutrons that sets off the chain-reaction – which –'

'How does the cross-section scale with energy?' Merriman interrupted.

Groves continued on a more practical level. 'What kind of explosive power are we talking about?'

'Before we answer that we've got to test critical mass and we can't begin that until we get some –'

'We need processed U235 or plutonium,' added Oppenheimer. He had edged across to the group to catch the last words.

'Thank you, Oppie. We have to experiment to see exactly how much material we need to create a chain-reaction and, er, an explosion.'

'How much of this stuff do you need?' asked Groves.

Merriman slipped in. 'We're projecting on a device of 30 pounds.' He was immediately accepted as part of the group.

'Right. Now, 30 pounds is as far away as the moon,' Groves sighed.

'If I've got these figures right, then 30 pounds of sub-critical material – that would give us . . .' Merriman's pencil worked away furiously, but Oppenheimer got there first.

'An explosion of the magnitude of 20,000 tons of TNT.'

'That's a very big bang,' Serber added.

Oppenheimer glanced across at the new boy and gave him a wink.

'So, shake out the bad news, I'm used to losing sleep.' Groves threw the problem at Oppenheimer, a challenge.

'We've got two problems. The first, detonation. The gadget disintegrates before it explodes. And second, weight. This method we've chosen – the gun method Bob was talking about, well, if we gamble with that, we've got a problem with the weight of the whole contraption. To fire a slug of material at the velocity necessary to send these elements critical, we need to construct something so big we wouldn't be able to lift the gadget with an industrial crane.'

'Deke?'

From out of the smog stepped Captain William

'Deke' Parsons. A navy man who had been assigned to the project by Groves because of his specialist knowledge of explosives, Parsons was what they called a 'straight navy' man. He had little time for theories, he just knew what worked.

'If they're talking about a diameter of seven inches, we're looking at a barrel thickness of . . . at least four inches.'

'I hope you guys know the music. The way things are, we can't even hum the tune.'

Nothing any one of the 'eggheads' had said sounded remotely practicable to Groves. And Parsons' expression condemned them all.

Oppenheimer ploughed on. 'Oh, we'll find a solution. I've decided to form two groups – two specifics. One explores the weight problem, the other looks for alternatives. Free discussion, open it out – give it some air.'

Groves had heard enough. 'I'm not sure –'

'Excuse me, General.' Oppenheimer stepped across his bow and gestured to the rest of the room. 'Two groups. Deke and Seth, gun barrel. Rob, detonation,' he called.

Groves, knowing they would now get down to the nitty-gritty, grabbed himself another chocolate out of a bag in his pocket and left them to get on with it.

It was midnight before Robert eased himself into a chair at the dining table. Kitty had set out a series of candles in the adjoining living room, measured out a couple of brandies and put the glasses on the coffee table. As Robert gazed in front of him she moved quietly from candle to candle with a burning taper. Then she collapsed on the couch. It was an invitation for Robert to join her. Instead, he reached across to the centre of the table and dragged a blackened *crème brûlé* towards him. He picked up a spoon and tapped the surface.

'Stop it,' she said.

'I believe this *crème brûlé* could make an excellent contribution to the national defence.'

'Stop it right now!'

'I'll have the staff have a look at it – it could make perfect armour-plating for a tank.'

'It got stuck in the oven.'

Robert raised his head and tried to make sense of her words.

'Look. The door wouldn't open.'

'The heat makes the metal expand – that's probably why,' he explained, getting to his feet. Kitty plumped up the cushions on the couch and he sank into them.

'I know why the door wouldn't open, but that didn't help me to open it.' She passed him his brandy, picked a cigarette out of the box on the coffee table and nuzzled up against him. She moved her head close to his ear and turned on her Marlene Dietrich accent. 'Got a match, soldier?'

It was very good. It ought to be, it was the accent her parents spoke with.

'*Bitte, Fräulein.*' Robert fished out his lighter and snapped the flame into life.

Kitty took a deep puff and was about to continue the impersonation when the front doorbell rang. For an instant she wondered whether there was some kind of conspiracy against her. Actually, the doorbell had just been a warning, for the door immediately swung open and Merriman came striding into the hallway.

'We're in here.'

'Jesus, Robert.' Kitty exhaled with a snort.

Merriman slipped sideways into the living room, closely followed by an older man, another of Oppenheimer's former students, Dr Seth Neddermeyer.

'Forgive us for disturbing you, sir, but – Look, we were listening to Serber talking just now and Seth here suddenly came up with something. I didn't think it could wait.'

Oppenheimer looked across at the tall gangling man, still half shrouded in the shadows. He stepped forward shyly and said, 'Implosion.'

Oppenheimer leaned forward, his eyes suddenly blazing. 'Go on.'

'I was thinking of an orange, of jumping up and down on an orange and crushing it.'

'Crushing an orange and crushing the core. Of course! Where are the others?'

'Up at Fuller Lodge. They want to kick it around.'

'Perhaps it can wait till –'

But Kitty had got up from the couch and made her way between them. 'That's all right. You go.' From the hall she called over her shoulder: 'I'd have lost you anyway.'

Robert followed her into the hall and gently took hold of her arm. 'Thank you,' he whispered. She smiled and nodded.

Then, when the house was empty again she stepped back into the candle-lit living room. It had not been as easy as all that and now she felt the emptiness surround her.

'Goddam,' she said clearly. Then, enunciating every letter: 'God-*damn*!'

*

Later that night it rained hard, so that in the morning the ground was like an unbaked pudding. The scientists were scheduled to be at the nearby explosives test-site to witness a series of experimental bombing flights. The site was reached via a long dirt road from the township. It, along with the entire countryside, had been turned into a quagmire. Some way down the road a convoy of vehicles was stranded. The cause of the problem lay at its head: the bus taking the scientists was completely and utterly bogged down. Groves stood up in his jeep, saw the problem and motioned to his driver to take him to it. A team of men had already got to work with shovels, while a row of faces at the windows of the bus watched with wide-eyed fascination. As Groves' jeep passed the bus he signalled to Oppenheimer to get out and join him. Oppenheimer stood at the door and looked down at the sea of mud. He glanced back at his colleagues who had the look of pupils watching as one of their number was about to be disciplined. There was nothing for it; he dropped down into the mud and waded across to the general.

'You had a meeting last night. I want to talk to you about it.' Oppenheimer had no idea what to expect, whether Groves was displeased or neutral. 'For the moment, yours are the only ears I want to pin back, all right?'

Oppenheimer shrugged.

'Listen, Doctor, please. Last night you guys discussed the work in public.'

'We were discussing an alternative to the gun method.'

'But in public, Doctor!'

'It was a table at the back, half a dozen of us . . . I'm sorry, I –'

'It is beyond forgiveness.'

'We were having a free discussion.' He delivered each word, slowly and deliberately.

'But I don't want free discussion. Look, the rules are we don't allow even a sniff of what we're doing here to leak out. That means compartmentalization. I don't want the theoreticians to know what the engineers are doing. I don't want the technicians to know what ordnance are doing.'

'That's crazy. You have no idea how science works. We must all have full access to all information, it's the only way we'll get results. If each person doesn't know what everyone else is doing, we'll end up duplicating work.'

Groves had no problem with the logic of the argument, it was the method. 'I'm aware of that, Doctor. Look, from now on discussion only happens in strictly designated areas. Information must be compartmentalized! And no one but you and the heads of divisions have unrestricted access. That's the way I want it. Get it?'

The tenor if not the details of their conversation drifted across to those in the convoy. De Silva beamed delightedly, while the scientists sighed in exasperation.

'Those kids came up with a beautiful idea last night. If only you'd been there. Neddermeyer's idea was brilliant. An explosion that goes inwards, an implosion creating a uniform compression of the core. No gun barrel, no weight problem, no velocity problem.'

The general did not understand the technicalities of

much of what Oppenheimer was saying to him, but it was clear that this had been a breakthrough. Oppenheimer stepped up to the jeep. 'If I'm going to run this project, General, then I do it on my terms. Free discussion, free access to ideas. Without it we will never reach your deadline.' Groves took a deep breath, but the boy wonder was off again. 'Now, we take a small amount of material, shape it into a ball, about the size of an orange, cover it with a layer of TNT, ignite the TNT and the material inside implodes and – Wham! So I'm going to let it run. I know we can't afford diversions, but this one I'm going to allow room to breathe.'

'Just don't give it to the waitresses,' snapped Groves.

They reached the test site around noon and by mid-afternoon the party had spread itself out across a wide stretch of the mesa. Tall, wispy aerials dotted the rough countryside, linked to each other by coils of black cable. The cables travelled up and over the contours of the land towards a couple of tents. Here soldiers gathered around radios in deep concentration. Scattered among the rocks Oppenheimer's men sat hunched over clipboards filled with figures, while a number of under-occupied soldiers stood with their hands on their hips, shaking their heads at the incomprehensible concerns of the scientists.

At the highest point, where the jeeps had been parked, Groves and a couple of military observers stood peering out through binoculars at the desert before them. Gradually the sound of aircraft engines filled the shallow canyon. Groves glanced at his watch and cursed them for being nearly 45 minutes late.

Through the glasses he could see two or three medium-sized bombers heading towards them. He glanced down at Oppenheimer, but he was absorbed in conversation with Neddermeyer.

'Here come your aircraft.' Oppenheimer glanced up and nodded to Groves. Then he and Neddermeyer climbed up to join the general. Oppenheimer could see he was waiting for an explanation.

'The point is, the gadget – when we get it – will be detonated at altitude. If it explodes on the ground, most of the effect will be absorbed by the earth. We have to develop a detonating procedure that will trigger the gadget at a height of about 1,500 feet. That way we'll get the maximum spread. Now, we're trying out all kinds of detonating mechanisms; some that respond to radar signals, some to barometric pressure and some to a simple internal clock.'

'OK, we got something happening up there,' came a voice from one of the tents. Straight ahead of them, a bomber had levelled out in preparation for the bomb run.

'Four seconds from drop, if it works,' said Neddermeyer. Through binoculars they watched a small, barrel-like object tumble from the plane. Across the bombing range, men with stop-watches began internal countdowns.

'Four, three, two, one . . .'

'No go,' said Oppenheimer.

From out of one of the tents a radio operator emerged. 'Should have gone, sir.'

Suddenly the drum shattered into fragments and moments later a faint crack echoed across the mesa.

'Michael?' Neddermeyer looked to Merriman.

'No. That was the barometric switch.' At that moment, the lead aircraft soared over their heads, wings waggling in farewell.

Behind him were another two aircraft, the first of which had settled into its run. While most eyes had been up on the clouds, Groves had been concentrating down, across the ground. There in the distance two jeeps streaked across the pitted bombing range.

'What the . . . What are they doing? Get them outta there!' A group of soldiers leaped into an empty jeep and started down the range. Meanwhile, those left on the hill waved furiously at the approaching lunatics.

Oppenheimer peered through the binoculars. 'It's Fermi. Something's up.'

Then one of the observers, concentrating on the approaching aircraft, shouted, 'What the hell! He's turning, sir!' The approaching aircraft aborted its run and banked away.

'He thinks we're waving him off,' explained the radio operator.

'Holy smoke, get them back!' said Groves explosively.

'Can't do that, sir.'

'*What?* I wait out here in the middle of nowhere for aircraft that are late, and then the goddam detonator misses! Now this,' he bawled, jabbing his finger at the approaching jeeps. 'Get those planes recalled!' As the radio operator jumped back into his tent, the first jeep pulled up at the command post. Out of the vehicle tumbled Enrico Fermi and a group of soldiers, each one furious with all the others. The first to get a word out was the military commander of Los Alamos, Whitney Ashbridge.

'I'm sorry, but it's an emergency. Work at the lab is at a standstill. Mr Farmer has been arrested. I told him not to come out here.'

Fermi headed straight for Oppenheimer, he wanted nothing more to do with the men in khaki. 'Oppie, this cannot go on. I cannot work under this –'

At that moment the tent flap opened again and a beaming radio operator announced that the flight was returning to complete its run. No one was interested, so he returned to his radio.

'This is ridiculous, Oppie. They've arrested me. Why?'

Groves looked at Oppenheimer, who returned the smallest of shrugs.

'Enrico – take it slowly. Colonel Ashbridge, why was Professor Fermi arrested?'

Groves and his observer had taken up their binoculars again as the drone of approaching aircraft made conversation more and more difficult.

'Mr Farmer exited without a pass.'

'*Dio Porco! Fermi*, my name is *Fermi*. Not Farmer. Why do I need a pass? Is this a prison?' asked Fermi. But the rest was lost. Suddenly the aircraft was upon them. Low, very low. It straightened out and appeared to have targeted the little hill where they all stood.

'It's too low. What's he doing, goddam it!' The radio operator bellowed into his microphone, 'Abort! Abort!' but the aircraft continued, released its bomb and banked away across the hills, ignored. Everyone concentrated on the bomb that it had left behind. It plummeted towards the earth, bounced about fifty feet in front of them and flew back into the air. The MPs in the second jeep scattered in every direction as the device returned to the earth. It crashed into the ground and finally came to rest beneath an empty jeep. Everyone had long since hit the dirt and was waiting, breath held. Groves called across to the chief weapons specialist.

'Deke?'

'Sir.'

'Will it detonate?'

'Ah,' Parsons took a bleak look at the device, 'no, sir.'

'Right.' Groves turned to the audience of scientists. 'In my office in an hour.'

SIX

'General Groves, you must understand that we are people, not numbers.'

'Not numbers . . .' The first obstacle was a determined floor-show, mounted by Fermi. The delegation had got to the office long before Groves had, and had already rehearsed their speeches. Groves had paused only to collect a fresh bag of chocolate and then had swung himself behind the big desk.

Neddermeyer came forward. 'It's just not part of our agreement.'

'And look, about your plans: barbed wire, why barbed wire?' Fermi had assumed the role of spokesman, and beside him stood Robert Wilson – the head of a group of theoreticians from Princeton – Neddermeyer, Teller and just about everyone else. Groves was flanked by de Silva, Latrobe, Pash, Ashbridge and a smattering of MPs. Oppenheimer stood with his back to the proceedings, staring out the window, while Groves, from the desk, let the arguments run on.

'Dogs,' chimed in Wilson.

'Dogs,' echoed Fermi.

'Guards . . .'

'Guards . . .'

'Watchtowers . . .'

'Even watchtowers!'

Groves's eyes had glazed over and he couldn't even be bothered to nod any more.

'. . . security badges. It's an intolerable atmosphere. You people don't appreciate that it is impossible to work under these conditions.' Franz Goethe had wanted to get rid of the security badges. They had always been his bugbear.

But Fermi hadn't finished. 'Yes, and secrets. I thought I'd left all this behind in Italy, with Mussolini.' Fermi indicated the attendant MPs.

'Oh, come on, Enrico,' Teller groaned from the baritone section. 'That's a bit farfetched.'

But Fermi ploughed on. 'General, openness, free exchange of ideas, it's a matter of principle for all scientists.'

'And there's more.' Goethe was at the bar again. 'I resent having my mail censored!'

Neddermeyer, meanwhile, had decided to become the voice of reason. 'General, these conditions will *not* help the project.' He glanced up at de Silva. 'We need your cooperation.'

Wilson had shaken off his partner and lunged towards the desk. 'The FBI talking to me is one thing, but to my wife and my neighbours . . .'

'Security badges! Secrets! *Dio mio!*' And with that, Fermi tossed his security badge on to Groves's desk. It was soon joined by others. Groves looked down at these tributes of academic defiance, swivelled out from behind his desk, tapped Oppenheimer on the shoulder and nodded towards the side door. Oppenheimer turned and looked at his colleagues. He raised his hand in a mute sign of solidarity as he went out.

Groves marched across the outer office, out to the veranda and took a deep breath. He leaned against the railing and waited for Oppenheimer to join him. 'That is a monkey-house! What are you going to do about it?'

Oppenheimer shoved his hands into his pockets and took in the view. By late afternoon the air seemed to have settled gently on to the mesa. Faint breezes stirred the treetops. He shrugged. 'Do about it? Well, I warned you. Look, it's simple. Give me complete autonomy in the lab areas. No compartmentalization.' Groves had his answer ready, but Oppenheimer hadn't finished. 'No compartmentalization: we move about as we like, where we like, when we like. I'll take responsibility for lab security. Outside the lab, you're in charge.' The general sucked at his teeth thoughtfully. 'I can sell them that, but that's all,' said Oppenheimer. 'Do we have an understanding?'

Groves knew that with that promise, he had Oppenheimer where he wanted him – there was no going back. But he pretended reluctant acquiescence: 'I don't like it, but I can live with it,' he grumbled.

The general walked down the stairs. Now he knew – Oppenheimer could be handled.

That evening the Oppenheimers threw one of their famous spur-of-the-moment parties: good food, some alcohol and lots of music to chase away the tension. Everyone came with their security passes, but not a word was spoken about them then or ever again. Edward Teller entertained them with renditions of Chopin on the old upright piano, others gathered around the radio and tuned into Santa Fe for news of the war. Out in the kitchen the general had been invited to apply his military know-how to the recalcitrant oven door. He knelt before it while Kitty stood over him. The general had already noticed that she was wearing a little too much makeup – and a little too much alcohol.

'What do you mean, am I enjoying it here?' she asked, and she let rip with a deep, dry laugh.

Groves tried to keep his mind on the oven. 'The thing's stuck.'

Kitty acted as if this were a revelation. 'It's the heat,' she explained. 'It makes the metal expand. I said it was badly designed.' She went on with scarcely a pause: 'How can I be enjoying myself? I hardly ever see my husband, we rarely even talk. I get lonely.'

'Well, we are fighting a war, ma'am. There's not much opportunity at the moment to go off to Acapulco.' Groves took hold of the handle, now red-hot, got to his feet and gave it an almighty wrench. The entire stove lifted off the floor and then the oven door came away from its hinges. Teller's rendition of the Minute Waltz scampered and crashed to a climax just as Groves completed his own noisy party-trick.

'Sorry about that, ma'am,' he said, looking at the wreck.

'Thank you, General,' Kitty said cheerily. 'Another few minutes and everything would have been overdone.' He shot her an evil glance but it failed to penetrate the liquor haze that surrounded her.

'I'll have this seen to.' He lowered the door to the floor.

'Don't worry about it. I'm sure we're going to be allies, General . . .' Groves looked up. He didn't understand the woman at all. 'We're both trying to seduce the same man,' she explained, as if to a child. She let a glazed smile drift across her face while Groves's cheeks blazed with indignation. 'So, is there a Mrs Groves?' she went on.

'Yes, of course there is.' He tucked his shirt in and hitched up his trousers. 'And she has the courage to stay in the background. Some men are in the world for a purpose, Mrs Oppenheimer. A good wife recognizes that, and she is happy to smooth the way. I hope we'll be allies, too.'

In the living room Oppenheimer was seated on the floor, surrounded by colleagues and admirers. He pulled away the cellophane on his fifth pack of the day and shook out a cigarette for Merriman. The young physicist shook his head.

'I've read a lot of your papers. Just marvellous.' Oppenheimer drew deeply on his cigarette. 'Especially your paper on the collapse of a star.'

'This is very hopeful. It didn't generate much enthusiasm elsewhere.' Oppenheimer tumbled his lighter around in the palm of his hand and looked interested, while his mind roved. He was glad they were all letting off steam, but he wanted to be somewhere else – real bad. Merriman had only just begun.

'I am very grateful you asked me to be here, sir. It's a real pleasure. Physics doesn't go over too big in Jackson, Illinois. They don't appreciate science for what it is.'

Oppenheimer's gut turned, but he nodded sagely. Of course he understood.

'So. You really find my theory on degenerate matter

interesting?' Merriman felt redeemed. 'Your model for the neutron-core collapse is just breathtaking.'

'I'm delighted. What do you think we're going to find here, at the end of the tunnel? A martini?'

They'd warned him about Oppie's blade: don't suck up to him, he's got no time for it. Merriman sank his face into his glass and tried to hide his blush. But then there was a burst of noise from the door and they all turned to see Shoenfield, Kathleen and Babyface making a rowdy entrance. In an instant all reason had escaped him and a smile slid slowly across Merriman's face. Oppenheimer saw his opportunity and slipped out of the room.

As he opened the door his den was flooded with light and the sound of Teller's Chopin. He shut it out again and stepped into the gloom. A full moon sent a cold, blue beam through the venetian blinds and across his desk. He picked up the phone and dialled the operator. When he spoke, it was in a cracked whisper.

'Hallo, operator? Let me have long distance. Berkeley 5558. Thank you.' The number rang and she answered. 'Hallo, Berkeley 5558?'

There was nothing at the other end, then a click as the line suddenly went dead. 'Hallo, operator? Operator, I . . . Yes, cut off. Could you try the number again? Thank you.' Same again. The number rang and she answered.

'Hallo, Jean? It's me. I know you're there.'

At last a faint, exhausted voice. 'Ah. I'd given up waiting.'

'Jean, I'm sorry. I couldn't manage before.'

'Robert, I was frightened. You didn't call, didn't write. Nothing. Not even a message.'

'I can't, Jean.'

'Can't? Why can't you? Tell me where you are at least. Robert, I'm paralysed without you.'

'No, Jean, I can't. My love, listen to me . . .'

Teller's piano echoed across the wooden slatted roofs, to a small hut in the military compound. There, late into the night, the defenders of the nation's security listened in on the lives of their neighbours. As the operator had tried the number, the guy on duty nudged his sleeping colleague. 'We got a long-distance on domestic, 212.'

'The professor.' He snapped a switch on the old wire-recorder. The first guy logged the time and the number called. Jean's voice trickled out from their Bakelite earphones.

'Why did you call?'

'Because I love you.'

'Oh. Are you coming home? *When* are you coming home?'

The guys in the hut looked at each other and sucked hard on their cigarettes. This dame means trouble.

In his den, the moonlight on Robert's face had carved a tortured mask.

'Jean . . .'

'We're not talking, we're just making noises. Why don't we just grunt at each other? Oh, excuse me, I know you've got to run, there's a war to win!'

'Jean, Jean, please. You've got to understand.'

But she was somewhere else, deep inside herself; there was no reaching her. 'I can't remember a day when I wasn't hurting, except when I was with you.'

'I love you, Jean.' But then the phone went dead

again and Robert was left holding the lifeless thing in his hand. He dragged his fingers through his hair and was on the verge of calling the operator again when the door swung open. He slammed the receiver down and turned to see a couple silhouetted in the doorway.

'Sorry, is – Dr Oppenheimer?'

'Yes.'

'Oh, sorry. We were just looking for our coats.'

'Sure.' His heart thumping like a drum, he slipped quietly back to the party. He stood watching from the corner of the room. Groves emerged from the kitchen, signalled that he'd had enough and was going. Oppenheimer waved to him, then leaned against the wall and let the noise wash over him as he watched everyone having a good time.

It was gone midnight when the newly promoted Major de Silva slipped the transcript into his briefcase. Outside Groves's house the crisp crunch of the sentry's boots mingled with the sound of the cicadas. As de Silva approached the general's door he tossed them a salute, which they returned. He dropped his cigarette to the ground, checked his watch and then tapped gently. He listened for a while, then knocked again. He checked his watch a second time and thought better of knocking a third time. As he stepped down off the porch the door swung open and there framed in the doorway was the fat man in his vest and pants.

'I'm sorry to disturb you, sir. De Silva.'

'What is it?'

'I won't keep you, General . . .'

'There had better be a good reason for you to be banging on my door at two in the morning.' Groves disappeared into the house and de Silva realized that this was as close to an invitation to enter as he was going to get.

'I had this typed up, sir. I thought you'd want to see it right away.'

Groves snapped on a standing lamp and held the sheet under the shade. 'What is this?'

De Silva ran his eyes around the living room. Spartan. He could see two simple armchairs, two open suitcases and a uniform laid out for the morning. He stepped up to the general's shoulder. 'I think she's working him over. I've seen it before.'

Groves looked up from the page and stared deep into de Silva's eyes. 'Who is this woman – this Jean?'

'Jean Tatlock. She's a known Communist.' Groves curled the page up and tapped the back of his hand with it.

'Get me her background. Maybe I'm missing something on the good doctor.'

'I feel that this has got to throw his entire position on the project into doubt.'

'Dr Oppenheimer *is* this project.'

'With respect, sir, this makes him an unacceptable risk.'

Groves shoved the paper back at de Silva and shepherded him to the door. 'You're wrong. Failure is the only serious risk. All that concerns me is that if he's with her he's not with us. I'm going to make it my personal responsibility to assure myself of his loyalty.'

De Silva stepped out on to the stoop and then paused. 'I think I have a right to know how you intend doing that, sir.'

'Wrong again, Major. You don't.'

And the door closed as Groves mimed inner satisfaction.

The following morning broke clear and bright. Out on the recreation field the scientists were taking on the military at a game of baseball. Both sides had scores to settle, and by the fourth inning, it was Army 3, Eggheads 2. Merriman had spent the morning in centre field and had just left to visit the men's room across the street.

He dodged the water truck making its way up the street. Everyone would be damn glad to see that water-tower finished. He cut across to the opposite curb and just missed Shoenfield coming in the opposite direction on his dust-coloured Harley-Davidson. Shoenfield swerved into the middle of the road and braked. 'For God's sake, Michael, watch where you're going!'

'I was, you lunatic. Why weren't you?' Shoenfield kept the machine at a crawl beside Merriman, but his attention was on a flock of WACs standing by the curb. 'I was, and that's where I'm going.' He gunned the engine and flashed them a romantic smile.

'Oh . . .'

'What do you mean, "Oh"? What's the point of my miserable experience unless there's a little bit of – Oh-oh. Just look at that!' Merriman did and shook his head.

'See, I don't get you, Michael – unless you're saving yourself for Kathleen Robinson.' Merriman didn't pause in his stride. 'She's definitely saving herself for you, pal.'

'Me?'

'Yeah. Can't see it myself, but seems you've got the inside track.'

'Come on.'

'Well, it's either you or me, pal.'

'Go on, get lost.'

Shoenfield slipped the machine into second and opened the throttle, hanging out a crazy wave as he left.

Inside the toilet block Merriman was confronted by the bulk of General Groves standing at one of the stalls. He stepped up beside him and unbuttoned his flies.

'Morning, sir.'

'How's it going? Seen the boy wonder?'

Merriman looked down at what he was doing and kept the conversation brisk. 'He's having a hell of a time and he's taking it out on himself . . .'

'Where is he?'

'In his office, I think.' Merriman refastened his buttons.

'Great. Don't forget to wash your hands, kid.'

'Bad time?' Groves tapped on Oppenheimer's open door and slipped his head through the gap. Oppenheimer was running over Wilson's figures on the velocity of the uranium slug for the gun-type bomb. Beside a blueprint of the device pinned to the blackboard he scribbled calculations that he was attempting to cross-check. If weight and mass could be determined on paper, it might save a great deal of time in conducting expensive trials with the actual material. But it was proving difficult – maybe impossible.

'Could be better. Trying to figure out the correct velocity, against weight and mass . . .' He tossed a broken piece of chalk away in frustration. 'Presenting a bit of a problem.'

Groves edged into the room and perched himself on the desk. He didn't bother to beat about the bush. 'Who's this dame you're running around with?'

Oppenheimer hadn't heard him. He was still wrapped up in the mass of Uranium 235. Then, 'What?'

'The dame you called the other night.'

Oppenheimer stared at him and wondered if he'd missed something. Groves stared straight back, making sure he had made himself clear. 'Do I have to spell it out to you?' queried Groves.

It wasn't possible. It just wasn't possible, Oppenheimer kept telling himself. In a split second a dozen possibilities raced through his imagination. Had someone come into the den? Heard him? One of his colleagues? Would they have talked to Groves?

'I got it on the QT from someone who owes me. But what happens if the next guy doesn't owe me? He gives it to the wrong person and that would be the end of you. And it would also be the end of the project.' Groves heaved himself off the desk. A steely light glinted in his eye. 'I don't understand you. Are you some kind of bohemian or something? I've been blind-sided! I never expected to be blind-sided by someone like you . . .' All Oppenheimer could do was stare at the man, unbelieving.

Groves had dropped his bombshell and felt it would reverberate more fully if he left Oppenheimer to deal with the implications by himself. He gave the younger man a pained shrug and left, well pleased with his morning's work.

When he got back to his office Groves moved quickly across to his window, the better to enjoy the sight of the boy wonder loping painfully past the baseball diamond towards the Admin Block and Groves's own office. He barged straight past a smirking Bronson and the general's secretary, who were expecting him, but before he could sit, Groves had turned and was blazing away at him.

'What about me in this? How do you think it reflects on my ability to choose the right people?'

Oppenheimer was exhausted. His mind flailed about for some handle on the thing. 'It was going on long before I became involved here. This is not a new thing. It is something in my private life, and it has nothing whatever to do with you or anyone else here.'

'I appreciate your candour, but it's not enough. I and my establishment cannot tolerate this situation, whether you think it concerns us or not. You don't seem to appreciate that this might quite possibly sink us all.'

'What are you talking about? This is a woman I care about . . .'

Groves slammed his hand down on the desk in front of him. 'She's a Communist! A *Communist*! It would be bad enough if she were a sweet young thing from Indiana, but a card-carrying Communist? How could you think – in your job, a classified job! What do you want me to do, draw you a map?'

Oppenheimer heard him clearly, but the general spelled it out just the same: 'I'm talking about getting you removed from this project.'

Oppenheimer slowly lowered himself into the chair. He felt beaten. It wasn't just Jean – and Kitty. It was the gadget. Groves had sucked him into the middle of this game, and now there was no way out. As Groves had foreseen from the moment he had heard of the phone call, he had the advantage. He leaned across the desk. 'Just get on the phone, use a safe line and tell her goodbye.'

At that moment, as if to add an exclamation mark, the office window shattered and splinters of glass flew across the floor. Oppenheimer dived off his chair while Groves went for the silver-plated Colt .45 in the cupboard. Then through the broken window came the whoops and cheers from the baseball diamond. Merriman had just smashed in a home run for the Eggheads. Bronson burst into the office just as Groves picked up the baseball. 'Relax, Bronson, we're all going to live.' He hefted the ball in the air a couple of times, then tossed it across to Oppenheimer. 'A different game, but I guess the ball is in your court.'

SEVEN

o

Groves's army Buick bucked and weaved down the rutted track. Accompanying the visiting general on his round of major operations were Pash and de Silva. As Bronson steered the vehicle into every pothole in the road, they were tossed around like grapefruit in a crate. The Buick weaved in and out of a convoy of trucks, loaded with curious steel contraptions, hoops and arches that formed the structures of Neddermeyer's experiments. They watched these almost prehistoric shapes pass by the windows and were none the wiser. Neddermeyer's concept of implosion had seemed the sweetest of all possible solutions, but it proved to be the most difficult actually to produce. The work continued through into 1944 with little sign of success. Out in the testing field, Neddermeyer worked with Deke Parsons to devise a way of coating a sphere of U235 with an explosive charge which, when detonated, would compress the sphere inwards equally from all sides. Could it actually be done? Groves was there to see results. De Silva wanted to be somewhere else altogether.

'Tatlock graduated 1932. The affair was broken off at that time and everything got put on the back burner until 1942.'

*

The major had taken the opportunity of a few moments alone with Groves to show him a file that they had been putting together on Oppenheimer and Jean Tatlock. The general shuffled through a sheaf of photographs of the couple while de Silva ran through the headlines: she had involved Oppenheimer in a number of political activities, with various anti-fascist, anti-Franco groups during the 1930s, when he became acquainted with a lot of Communists.

During this litany, Groves shuffled through his protégé's intimate past. There were pictures of political rallies, a meeting of a women's group in an open-air restaurant, Oppenheimer and Tatlock together at the beach. Groves had been getting angrier and angrier as he looked at the file.

'Bronson! Less muscle on the gas!' he yelled as the car hit a particularly deep rut.

'Sir?'

'Colonel Pash has a mission coming up in a couple of months. I want him to get started while he's still alive.' Bronson took the admonition with a grin and eased off the gas. Meanwhile, de Silva still had an issue to settle.

'Surely this makes Oppenheimer a sitting duck for blackmail. I must demand his removal from the project.'

'Forget it, Major. Now, you just relax and enjoy the drive.' De Silva was a man who owed his promotion to this project. His chief had filled the general's ears with praises for the young captain, and now that he'd been made a major, de Silva saw Oppenheimer as his ticket back to Washington. If he could land this fish, his career would be made.

'Look, Peer, I appreciate your sense of responsibility, and so far as I'm concerned you're doing a great job. But on this issue, I think I know the best approach.'

'For what it's worth, General, I think de Silva's right. I think he's as red as –' Pash started to join in, but Groves cut him short.

'OK. Let's get this over with once and for all. Look, I know you guys talk among yourselves, but so far as I'm concerned, Boris, you're straight Intelligence. Leave security matters to de Silva. I know you're going to do a great job for us once you get to Germany. I know the team you've picked is first class and you're going to do great. But that's what I want you to concentrate on: getting those German installations. The major is just hunting. He doesn't know his rabbit. Oppenheimer has got too much at stake.' Pash heaved a sigh and turned back to the window. Groves let the car rumble on for a moment, then he handed the pictures back to de Silva.

'We've all got a lot at stake here. You, me, Oppenheimer – all of us.'

'Do you think he's a loyal American?' asked Pash.

'He'd better be. Let me tell you, I know most of the longhairs on this project and I don't think any one of them could push this thing through in the time Oppenheimer can. All we need is to have the guy at heel, right? Now if that's what we want, then you don't drag a man by the nose, you just close off his options. Simple.' Groves produced a box of chocolates and offered them around. 'No marzipan.'

Out on the test site they let off another charge of

explosives and waited in the bunker while the dust and debris gradually settled around them. Neddermeyer was out of the bunker first to check the results, but the look on his face when he turned told the story. Another failure. Merriman had been pressed to the optical X-ray unit, observing the wave patterns. He looked up to show a mask of fine brown dust and a pair of clear circles around his eyes. Oppenheimer and Merriman clambered out to join Neddermeyer, who stood above the remnants of his theory, a figure of absolute despair.

'We could try a thinner wall and increase the compression,' Oppenheimer offered. 'There's an answer here somewhere.'

'Maybe implosion's a blind alley.'

'Try it, Seth. Cover every angle. When you've done that, then we'll call it a blind alley,' encouraged Oppie.

The three of them stood there, hands on hips, surveying the scene. Neddermeyer ran through his calculations again. He was close to giving up. Merriman watched a party of engineers moving towards the mound of soft sand where the explosives were set. At the rear, he caught sight of a straggler, clutching a bundle against his chest. Merriman slapped Neddermeyer on the back, 'Are we going again –' But the sentence was never finished. A sudden cold, sharp crack of high explosives shattered the conversation. Over where Merriman had been gazing there was now only a crumpled heap of khaki. The three of them ran towards the soldier sprawled awkwardly across the sand.

The khaki mound let out a cry that chilled everyone

who heard it. Merriman ran closer and saw the dark blood starting to pump from the boy's leg. The cries continued, on and on. Ahead of them, just arriving at the scene, another soldier stumbled to a halt and screamed, 'Get back! Get back!' He had the look of a doomed man. No more than ten feet away, among the tattered limbs and cloth, he had spotted the unexploded charges. 'For Christ's sake, we've got live ones here!'

His buddy's blood was turning the desert into thick, congealed mud. The man on the ground swallowed his pain and began to drag himself towards Merriman, away from the charges scattered in the sand. But he still clutched in his hand the charge he had forgotten to drop – and it was armed. Merriman and the soldier looked at each other. They knew that if they tried to disarm the charge, they'd probably both go. The soldier's chest was now soaked with blood, but the pain was in his leg. He dragged himself further from the other charges.

Merriman skirted the charges in the sand and stooped down to the injured soldier. Both their lives were balanced in the grip of a dying man. He had begun to shake with the cold that follows deep shock. Merriman knew that this could easily set off the second charge, but: 'Steady . . . steady,' and Merriman slowly closed his hands round the boy's bloodied fist and he tried to ease the charge away. 'I've got it. I've got it,' he told the boy. Oppenheimer made as if to move towards them, but Neddermeyer held him back. From where they stood they could see little of what was happening. All they knew was that the wounded soldier had stopped crying and that the other soldier stood paralysed, seemingly rooted to the spot. The wind blew angrily, whipping up the sand. Merriman's forehead ran with rivulets of sweat that gathered at his brows and stung his eyes. The boy's hands had stopped shaking, but now his lips were blue. Merriman wiped the sweat away with his forearm. Finally he had hold of the charge and looked up at the soldier standing above him, as if to say – What next? Oppenheimer saw none of this, just the puff of dust and sand as he heard another crack of explosives.

'Christ.'

Then out of the dust appeared Merriman and, cradled in his arms, the young engineer, bloodied but alive.

'It's OK . . . We're all OK.'

The ambulance had wailed across from its station nearby and the doors were already open by the time Merriman reached the bunker.

'Don't you ever fuckin' leave your post again,' bawled Parsons.

'Electrical failure in the detonating system,' someone said, and another mentioned something about lanthium contamination.

After the young engineer had been put into the ambulance, Merriman looked up to see Shoenfield and Kathleen in the back.

'I had no idea you guys . . .'

Shoenfield ran a Geiger counter across Merriman. 'Do me a favour, just jump in the back, will you? You guys play with some funny stuff, know what I'm saying? I want to give you the once over back at the hospital.' Merriman looked across at Kathleen. In return he got a warm, slow smile that filled his heart.

At the base hospital they found some minor burns on

the palms of Merriman's hands, which they bandaged loosely. As the soft evening light drifted into the ward, he sat on his bed drinking it in. He'd stopped writing in his diary – it was becoming painful – and turned at the sound of a woman's footsteps. It was Kathleen, bringing a cup of tea.

'Here.'

'Thanks.'

'What are you writing?'

'Oh, nothing. I can't send letters home, so I'm keeping a diary for my dad, for when all this is over.'

Kathleen moved across to the battered old gramophone by the window and shuffled through the stack of records. 'You took quite a risk out there.'

'Instinctive, that's all.'

She picked out a record and turned back to the patient.

'Instinct. It is still instinctive to save a man, with this war and everything? Then what makes us want to kill? Is that instinct too?'

'You sound like my dad. Always shootin' off questions like that . . .'

'What's he like?'

'He's a preacher. Jackson, Illinois. I have a brother, older than me – Jimmy. He's a soldier. Ma's dead. Dad's kind of hurt that I'm not at the front.'

'Why?'

'I couldn't tell anybody where I was going or what I was doing . . . except Box 1665, Santa Fe, New Mexico. See, Jackson's a real small town. When I left he said, "Boy, since you aren't going to be a soldier, be a damned good scientist. The best." ' She watched him closely as he spoke.

'Are you the best?'

'I was in Chicago. But out here, with all these guys, I don't know. Sometimes I think I'm way over my head. These guys, they're so bright. But I can handle anything they throw at me – so far.'

'But can you dance?'

'Pardon me?'

'Can you dance?'

'Are you serious?'

'Can't handle it?' His embarrassment lasted only a moment, and then he was on his feet. Kathleen dropped the record on to the gramophone and the needle on to the record. Suddenly his hands were around her waist. She turned to him, he moved her gently and they were dancing.

As night fell, a cold desert wind blew up from the south. Oppenheimer had called Franz Goethe, Volney Wilson and Parsons to a crisis meeting. He wanted to show them their progress on that ubiquitous flow-chart. Since he had first shown it to the scientists, Oppenheimer had gained a tan, but lost weight. The lines were etching themselves deeply into his face.

'We can't speed things up any more,' Goethe said flatly.

'Don't tell me that, Franz. Ten months into this thing and we are approaching a plateau. We can't let that happen, we've got to keep pushing onwards.' All about them stood dirty coffee cups and ashtrays overflowing with cigarette butts. The thin yellow glow from the overhead lights barely managed to cut through the smoke.

Dr Franz Goethe and Oppenheimer were no great

allies. They had known each other during their post-graduate studies in Germany, where Oppenheimer had taken pleasure in finding fault with some of Goethe's calculations. Oppie continued: 'Now if we want the physics to advance, then engineering had better get on the ball. We're behind on engineering.'

'Exactly. We can't advance the physics until we are working with something practical – until engineering is on the ball,' agreed Wilson. He had originally had strong moral doubts about the construction of an atomic bomb, but was persuaded by the probability that the Germans would soon have the same weapon. The two of them, Wilson and Goethe, often felt utterly overwhelmed by Oppie, and they avoided this kind of session if at all possible.

'We are fully stretched. We can't speed things up much more,' said Goethe again.

'The manufacture of plutonium and the separation of U235 is completely dependent upon the pace engineering sets here.'

'But Oppie, we just don't have the manpower.'

Oppenheimer opened his mouth to reply as the room was suddenly plunged into darkness.

'*Christ!* Why the hell can't this army keep the generators running?' Oppenheimer's nerves were stretched taut and this was just one more straw. In the darkness that consumed them Goethe and Wilson could almost feel the despair raging inside of their boss.

'Get the goddam lights on!' he screamed down the hallway. Outside the desert wind battled with the thin wooden structures scattered across the mesa. They all listened to the creaking eaves and crashing shutters, but there was no reply. They were alone in the building in the dark. Oppenheimer decided there was no point in prolonging the debate. He announced: 'We've got to accelerate the pace of development right alongside the theoretical. I'll get on the phone to Groves in the morning and double the staff if we have to. And I don't want to hear any more about domestic problems here at Los Alamos. I'll be damned if this project is to be brought to a halt because of a little mud in our tap water.'

Oppenheimer pushed his way through the wind, clutching a bundle of technical drawings under his arm. He steered himself towards his house, his mind swimming with the sheer scale of the project. He worried that it was spiralling out of control, that it was getting too big. As the four men had said goodnight to each other on the steps of his office, the street lights had suddenly come on again. They'd laughed, the tension draining away. With that problem solved, all that remained, Oppenheimer thought, was – well, everything else. He closed his front door behind him, pushing the sound of the storm down to a low howl. The sound of Gounod's *Faust* drifted across from the living room.

He was exhausted, he had no desire to do anything at all, so he just stood there listening and let the music curl around him. He hadn't played that old recording for years, not since before the war. Robert moved quietly to the living room and found Kitty in an armchair, a glass cradled in her hand and the cocktail shaker on the floor beside her.

'I just had that goddam Mrs Parsons on the phone. Another of her stultifying dinner parties next week.

She thinks that because her husband wears a uniform she's more important than anyone else.'

Robert picked up the shaker and swirled it around. There was enough for one more.

'I told her that my guests are more important than hers.'

'That's great, Kitty.' He poured himself a drink and swallowed it quickly.

'Heard the news tonight?' she asked. 'We fire-bombed Frankfurt last week.'

'We heard it last week.'

'Half the city's gone. They think 50,000 died.'

'Kitty, for Christ's sake, this place is a goddam mess.'

'This place is a goddam mess because there's no goddam water,' Kitty returned. 'There wasn't any today and there wasn't any yesterday.' She lifted her head and saw her husband, still clutching his bouquet of drawings. 'What do you want me to do, make water? The nurse had to take Peter to the bath-house, for God's sake.'

'I know, I know. That's all I've heard all day. Everybody had to go to the bath-house. Other wives manage, so why can't you?' She stared through the haze, her head nodding slightly. 'I'm sorry, Kitty.'

'Sure. You're tired. The strain is getting to everyone.'

'But everything rests on me.'

'Everyone says you're doing wonderfully, that you're the only one who could pull this off.'

He shrugged this aside, crossed to the table and spread out the drawings before him. Though she knew he was nearly dead with exhaustion, she couldn't hold back. There had really only been one thing that had gnawed away at her all day and it hadn't been the water.

'What time are you leaving tomorrow?'

That hit him. He had pushed it completely out of his mind and left it there to resurface when the time was right. Why should she ask about that now?

'She phoned,' said Kitty abruptly. 'I picked it up. The line went dead.' Kitty had surprised herself. Despite the numbing booze, she had begun to fall apart. 'You're going to see her again, aren't you? Aren't you, Robert?'

He slowly stood erect, placed his hands on his hips and arched his aching back, but the pain was deeper. His first reaction was to hate Kitty for it. He knew he had hurt her with his deception in the past, but now he was about to renounce all that.

'Goddam you!' she yelled. 'You are, aren't you?'

'Just to say goodbye, Kitty,' he said, with no feeling in his voice at all. 'It's over.' He turned to look at her. The toughness had melted, and she looked so very fragile.

'Because of me?' she whispered.

Robert reached out and folded her into his arms. He ran the question through his mind once again, and knew he couldn't answer. 'I love you,' was what he said instead.

'Robert?' She looked up into his face. 'I think I'm pregnant. Well, I don't know. We're waiting.' A weak, fragile smile crept across her face. There was nothing in Robert's eyes at all. Kitty wondered if he had heard. She reached up to him and gave him a long kiss.

'A baby? Peter said he wants a brother.'

She searched his face but the news hadn't sunk in. Or, if it had, it made no difference. Kitty knew there was no point in trying for more just then. She'd told him. That was enough.

'I'm going to get undressed and go to bed.' She swayed awkwardly towards the door.

'I won't be long,' he said, after she'd gone.

In his den he snapped on the desk light and unrolled one of his blueprints. There it was. Like Leonardo's dissection of a pregnant woman, the inner beauty of the gadget was revealed in loving detail. Beside it was the legend – 'Little Boy'.

Oppenheimer had asked Frank to pick him up at the Southern Pacific Station in San Francisco. Frank usually did whatever his brother asked. He'd been overshadowed by Robert's brilliance since they were children, and instead of trying to strike out in his own direction, Frank had decided to take up science as well. He'd always felt that all he would ever be able to do was look up to his brother and follow if he could. And follow he did. Robert had used his influence to get him a good position at the radiation lab out at Berkeley.

These thoughts rattled about in his head as he drove to the station. He rarely came down to the Mission district where to him the atmosphere of the nearby wharfs seemed to suggest the possibility of danger. He parked on Townsend, opposite the station entrance, and scanned every face that emerged on to the street. Oppenheimer's train got in from Santa Fe just after five o'clock, which meant that he would be somewhere in the homebound crush.

This seemed ideal to Robert. As he walked through the station concourse he was grateful for the sea of anonymous faces. On the pavement outside he held back from the curb, searching the street for Frank's car. Then he glanced over his shoulder to see if anyone was following him, and checked if there was anyone waiting casually on the street corner with a newspaper. When the lights changed he ploughed straight into the crowd, aimed for the opposite curb and slipped in through the open door of Frank's car. Then it all went wrong. The car wouldn't start. Frank turned the key again and again, praying for the engine to turn over, while passers-by idly turned at the sound.

'This is ridiculous!' said Frank desperately. 'Are we being followed or something?'

'Don't joke about it. I almost asked you for your ID.' They laughed with relief as the engine burst into life. As they swept down to the Embarcadero and under the Bay Bridge, Robert glanced over his shoulder at the following vehicles. His nervousness was infectious, and Frank too found himself constantly glancing in the mirror.

'They tap my phone, open my mail – God Almighty,' Oppie suddenly burst out. 'I get hounded for the names of anyone I know who might be a Communist – or have Communist sympathies. It's . . . it's . . .' He suddenly caught himself and looked across at his brother's expression.

'They know all about me, Robert,' said Frank quietly. 'They know I'm out of it.' They drove on to the next set of traffic lights and pulled to a halt. 'That place is like a prison. I don't know why you stay.'

Startled, Robert sat for a moment or two pondering

the question, then took another look over his shoulder. 'Well, I know it sounds crazy, but there's some order to it all. My life is normally full of chaos, but up there it's got an order. And I want to see the project through.'

'Why?'

Robert mocked himself. 'Well, they need me up there.' Frank swung the vehicle heavily around the next corner and then threw a look of impatience at his brother. 'And I like it. The work is extraordinary. It's such a sweet problem. They see me in a special kind of way. I need that, and I need them . . .'

'And Jean?'

Robert held up his hand to break the conversation off and Frank swallowed his words. A little further on he tested the water again. 'Listen, I was talking to some of the guys in Chicago.' Robert felt a frisson of anxiety and flashed a glance over his shoulder. Frank was sometimes allowed to visit Laurence's group at Oak Ridge and sometimes even came to Los Alamos. 'Szilard and some of the others are getting worried that the Russians are being left out of the picture. They're worried that it could turn into a threatening situation. You know, if one party's got something this big they answer to no one else.'

When he stopped there was nothing but the sound of the motor between them. 'I mean, they are our allies . . .'

'Jesus, don't start, Frank. I don't even want to know that you're thinking this. And I don't want to hear about Szilard. Here, let me out at the corner.' Frank nosed the car up to the curb and slipped into neutral.

'Will I see you later?'

'Sure. I don't know. Don't wait up for me.' Frank peered through the windscreen at the empty street, then leaned back in the seat and waited. His brother had cradled his head in his hands. He didn't seem to be weeping, and he might just have been tired, or he might be praying. Suddenly he looked up and squeezed Frank's shoulder. 'Take care.'

'You too.'

EIGHT

He took a table towards the back of the bar, by the windows, so that he could see everyone who entered. It was a little place on the Embarcadero, not far from Fisherman's Wharf, that he knew well. It seemed somehow appropriate. Over his shoulder he could see across the bay to Oakland and even the Berkeley Hills. Everything was out of kilter, but somehow focused, too. His old campus seemed at least a thousand miles away. Nothing he had done before appeared to be relevant anymore. The students, his old colleagues, the entire university community nestling at the foot of the hills, they were already insignificant. He was at the head of the greatest scientific adventure ever. Berkeley was history.

Then he was thrown from his lofty position by a vision – and she was a vision – standing in the doorway. Suddenly all the old songs were playing again. Jean looked astonishing. She swept up to his table and they both stumbled through apologies for being late. All his promises, all his decisions, hadn't meant a thing. All he could cling to at the moment was the extraordinary fire in her eyes as she looked unwaveringly at him. She had missed him so.

'I didn't get your message until about five. I was still at the hospital and I got all whizzed up into a huge panic.'

'You look wonderful.'

'You look so serious. What's the matter?' Robert glanced down and she watched him fidget with the matchbook on the table.

'Jean, we don't have much time. I'm going back tonight.'

'Tonight? But I was going to cook us dinner.'

'Ah ...' Robert hesitated – wavered. He looked down at the matchbook and turned it over again. 'Look, this can't be about dinner. I didn't want to tell you over the telephone. That's why I'm here.'

'What's wrong? What is it?' He finally managed to look up, his eyes swimming. Jean felt her stomach lurch, but she remained a picture of absolute calm. She picked up her napkin and smoothed it across her lap. She continued: 'I see. We're going to spill blood before we've even had cocktails. Is it because of what you're doing?'

Robert couldn't answer.

'You're going to hurt me, aren't you?' He heard Kitty's words again from the night before. 'I knew you would. Maybe that's why I came.' Her control began to crumble and she was on her feet, heading for the cloakroom. She had already slipped into her coat and was at the door by the time Robert reached her.

'Jean.'

'Please stay tonight. Please, please, *please*.'

He went with her, following an old feeling, one he thought he had quelled, but remnants of which clearly lingered. In her room, she ran her hands across his thin frame and thought how he seemed to have shrunk slightly. His face, neck and arms were now dark from the sun, but his chest was almost blue-white.

When they collapsed on to the bed they were flooded with familiar tastes and sensations. She held him down on his back and rolled over him, taking him slowly inside her, settling into a gentle rhythm. They looked only at each other's faces as they rocked back and forth in an old, sweet harmony.

When she came, she shuddered into a rigid arch, felt a streak of pain capture the pleasure and then she sank, with a sigh, on to his chest. She moved over and curled up at the edge of the bed, as taut as a steel band. There seemed to be no joy for either of them – just a commitment they couldn't be released from. A pause. Outside, the evening had vanished, street lights became brighter. The sounds of the traffic had sunk to a quiet swish.

'Robert,' she said finally.

'Hmmmm?'

'Would you tell me what is it you're working on? It's a bad thing, isn't it?' He shook his head. 'It *is* bad,' she continued, 'and that's why you can't tell me.'

'I can't tell you because it's a secret.'

'Tell me one good thing that's a secret.'

'*We* were good.'

Jean sat up and stared at him. 'No we weren't. Not when you got married. Robert, give me up for something I can understand. For Kitty or for Peter, for something that's alive – but not for a secret. Not for something in the dark.' She leaned over and kissed him. The sweat had begun to collect on her back and it glistened in the moonlight from the window. They slipped back into an embrace. He was not going home tonight.

Robert moved his hands across her body, rediscovering the shape that had been part of his life for so many years. She traced the contours of his face with her tongue – and soon they were united again. Gradually their love-making became urgent and she held him tightly, rolling him on top of her. He buried himself inside her, she cupping him in her legs, his face in her hands, like a drowning woman embracing the current.

As the morning crept in on them, the details of the room gradually filled out. All around were photographs of the two of them: at rallies for the unemployed, speaking at an anti-fascist meeting. His eyes flickered from one memory to another as Jean slept. Robert hadn't. He had dressed and was standing by the window. Jean slowly began to wake and then quickly sat up.

'Oh God, I dreamed you had gone.'

Robert moved the curtain slowly aside. Down in the street was a dark Chevrolet and in a doorway opposite a man was hugging his overcoat around him. Robert ducked sharply. Jean understood immediately, covered herself with her dressing-gown, crossed to the window and looked out.

'That's why the silences. No letters, no contact. I thought it was me.'

'I told you,' he said tonelessly.

Jean moved back to the bed. 'Yes, but . . . Robert, what *is* it you're working on? What is so goddam important?'

'It *is* important, so don't be so goddam righteous!' His anger had come as a shock. She was still not quite awake and was trying hard to fit things into the right spaces.

'Is it righteous to want to know where you are, what's happening to you? I just want to be close to you, to understand.'

'It's just . . . different now.' Robert was now caught up in anger of his own. They had followed him, they had dared to follow the director! Jean was now just so much flotsam.

But from deep inside her, the fire that had raged was now almost out of control. 'You bastard! I know why you're giving me up.' She waved a hand at the men in the street. 'Christ, we used to fight this kind of thing together!' She wrenched a picture of Robert from the dressing-table mirror and held it crumpled in her fist in front of his face. '*This* was the man I loved. The man I loved completely. I loved his dreams, I loved what he saw but couldn't prove.' He moved to her, but she cowered away from this stranger in her room.

'Jean, don't.'

'I loved the greatness in him. He was my proof that the world could be made better. He was good, and I was his. And if he's dead now, then I don't want to . . . to . . .' She was crushed. He reached for her.

'Please, Jean.'

'No!' She pulled away and he stood looking down at her. She was wracked with pain. Gradually she gained control and heaved herself up on one arm. 'I understand now. You mattered. You really mattered to me.' But he had gone, and when the door closed behind him there was a solid finality about the echo that filled the apartment.

A heavy shower was falling over the entire Bay area and the towers of the Bay Bridge were lost in the leaden sky. Robert hadn't spoken since he'd climbed into the car. They had passed San Bruno on the way to the airport before Frank broke the silence: 'Is she wrong?'

'So romantic . . . No. I don't know.' Robert tiredly pushed himself up in the seat and ran his fingers through his hair. 'When this is all over I want to spend six months just riding the mesa. No decisions, no deadlines . . . nothing.'

They pulled into the car park at San Francisco Airport as the final passengers were crossing the tarmac to Robert's plane.

'Thanks Frank . . . for being so reliable.'

Frank watched his brother running through the rain to the steps. Once Robert was gone he turned the car back towards the city. He didn't notice the Chevrolet parked by the exit.

In the clear air of New Mexico the ground gets baked hard and days pass without anyone ever seeing a cloud. Neddermeyer and Parsons were still attacking the problem of implosion. They had contrived ever weirder metallic shapes into which they placed their explosives, but with each failure they seemed to slip further from any solution.

Once again, as so many times in that summer of 1944, the men settled into their bunker, peering out at the gently rolling cattle country. At the turn of a switch the earth began to heave into the air and with it came an enormous boom that echoed back and forth across the mesa. As the thin brown earth swirled across the site Merriman, Neddermeyer and Oppenheimer strode towards the crater. Neddermeyer took out a handkerchief, picked up a piece of mangled steel tube and showed it to Oppenheimer. 'Look at it, Oppie. It's twisted, and it's got to be flat.' He tossed the shrapnel to the ground and wiped his forehead. 'I think implosion is just a pipe-dream. I'm sorry I ever thought of it. I just can't make it happen.' He looked at Oppenheimer for sympathy, but there was none. He tried again, tried to think calmly. 'Somehow I've got to focus the shock waves. Oppie, listen to me, I'm running out of ideas.'

But Oppenheimer's attention had been drawn to a jeep that had just pulled up beside them. Otto Frisch bounced out, still waving to them, then said, 'Oppie, Serber needs you back at the lab.'

Oppenheimer turned to Neddermeyer: 'Sounds to me like an excuse for not thinking. If you can't do this, Seth, if you're out of your depth . . .'

'No!'

'Just tell me and I'll get someone to help. You said it yourself. Focus. I know that somewhere there must be someone working on a way of focusing explosive shock waves.' He turned to the jeep. 'I'll find him. You just keep working.'

Merriman and Parsons watched the jeep bound away, trailing a veil of dust. 'If Oppie doesn't let up, he's gonna fall apart,' said Parsons.

Back at the lab, Robert took the stairs to his office two

at a time. Serber and Teller were waiting impatiently on the landing. They quickly ushered him into his room. With the door closed they looked at each other for a moment and then Teller blurted out: 'I'm sorry – you're probably going to wish you'd never set eyes on me.' Oppenheimer closed his eyes and waited. 'The good news is that the new plutonium from Hanford makes lots of neutrons. The bad news is that the spontaneous fission rate is much too high.'

Oppenheimer tightened his fists. 'Are you certain?' he said tightly.

'The reaction will run away with itself. There will only be a fizzle at best.'

'Shit!' He turned his back on them and punched his fists deep into his pockets. 'Who did the calculations?'

'Segrè.'

'Himself?'

'Emilio personally.'

Oppenheimer arched his back under the weight of this new setback. 'Oh God! If plutonium is a problem we may have to rely on U235. And of course Oak Ridge can't come up with anything like enough.' He looked across at Teller. 'That means we have to go with implosion.' Teller shrugged and Oppenheimer delivered *his* bad news: 'And Neddermeyer has just announced that he and implosion have just reached a brick wall.' Then he placed both hands on the desk and let his head fall between his shoulders. For an instant, he looked as though he might collapse. But he was still fighting. 'We can't fall behind. We just can't.'

'Oppie, are you all right?'

'Of course I am. We'll just have to go through that

brick wall. Do me a favour. Keep this quiet. I don't want it to get around the lab.'

In her kitchen Kitty was trying her best to make supper. Some of the boys were expected around seven. She and Robert had hardly spoken a word to each other since his trip to San Francisco, and she had filled up the silence with yet more booze. By now she had begun to drink before noon, so the evenings were really a blur. From the corridor she could hear Robert on the phone to the general. 'I don't care how much it's costing . . . Now wait a minute, General . . . Now just wait a minute. Don't you talk to me as if I haven't been giving this project all my attention, twenty-six hours a day, eight days a week. I've given up everything . . . I don't want to hear that from you. You know exactly what I'm talking about. I don't give a damn about restriction on my travel, it had to be done face to face and that's what I did.' As the phone came down with a crash, Kitty lifted her hand to wipe her eyes.

At the table Teller, Goethe and Merriman had run out of conversation. Kitty had been a lugubrious presence throughout, while Robert nudged at one problem after another as though he were examining sea-urchins in the shallows. The sound of cutlery on crockery played like a tattoo on their nerves.

'If,' said Robert through a mouthful of food. Merriman turned to him. 'If spontaneous fission is an impractical consideration, what then?' No one wanted to pick it up. Merriman looked across at Kitty and received a cold, polite smile.

'I've heard that people are considering contaminating the food supplies,' Teller noted.

'Yes. I asked Fermi to take a look at that report. He's suggesting Strontium 90. But it would have to affect at least half a million people to be worth a try.'

Kitty shrivelled at her husband's stone-like sensibility. Her only antidote was sarcasm. 'Well, why don't you put whatever it is you're making into a huge frankfurter, dangle the thing out of a bomber and then those Germans that aren't poisoned by it will break their necks trying to get a bite.' Merriman enjoyed that, but no one else was in the mood.

'I think Edward should play something on the piano,' Goethe suggested.

'How about the Funeral March?'

'Kitty.'

'Sorry. How insensitive of me! We need to be light. Only happy music here.' And with that she took her glass and moved to the piano. She placed the martini at the top end and then launched straight into 'I love all the many charms about you. Above all, I want my arms about you.' Kitty sang without taking her eyes from Robert. 'Don't be a Nazi, baby. Come to mama, come to mama, do, my sweet embraceable you.' She finished, raised her martini into the air and took a bow to absolute silence.

NINE

Operation Harborage had been thrown together at the last moment. It absorbed massive military resources and was one of the most absurd episodes in the European war. As Allied armies began to carve their way through German territory, the ALSOS operation to capture both the German atomic installations and its scientists moved into top gear. Colonel Pash's intelligence had pinpointed the town of Strausborg as the centre of the Nazi atomic laboratories. But to Groves's alarm the little town in southern Germany lay right in the path of General De Gaulle's advancing armies – the French might get there first. Pash had recommended a parachute assault on the town, an assault in which they would blow up the factories and perhaps even kidnap the scientists. Groves decided not to take any chances and an entire army corps was diverted across the French lines towards Strausborg.

The French, however, moved faster than expected and Pash was forced to send a single battalion ahead and catch up with them when he could. By the time the 1279th Combat Engineers had taken the town there was very little of it left. As Colonel Pash was driven down the main street he passed rows of buckled walls and mountains of rubble. Refugee children stood at an army mobile kitchen, while elderly couples pushed their belongings before them on wheelbarrows or bicycles. His driver weaved the jeep in and out of the craters that lay in their way and eventually slowed to a complete halt before the final obstacle, a grizzled lieutenant, standing in the middle of the road.

'Who the fuck are you?'

Pash's driver handed the lieutenant a piece of paper just as a burst of gunfire swept across the countryside.

'Ours,' the lieutenant said laconically. 'We're mopping up the next village.' He scanned the slip stamped SECRET and fell upon Eisenhower's signature. 'Well, what you're lookin' for is just up there.' He jerked his thumb towards a ruin. 'One of your guys has been with them since yesterday.' The lieutenant leaned into the jeep and checked a couple of wooden crates in the back marked 'fragile, Product of Belgium'. 'What's in the crates?'

'Chocolate. Two hundred pounds.'

'Hope she's fuckin' worth it.' The lieutenant's last words were cut off by the growing sound of an engine screaming above their heads, a scream that grew into a roar as a lone Stukka dive-bomber bore down on its target. Pash and his driver scrambled out of the jeep as the children scattered in all directions. Suddenly the square was empty.

'There's a box of grenades in the back,' the driver yelled as he shepherded everyone to shelter. 'This I don't want to see.' The Stukka made a direct hit. The bone-shattering explosion lifted the road and everything on it forty feet into the air. Fragments of jeep were sent flying in every direction. After the ear-splitting noise came the gentle sound of falling debris. Slowly Pash and the driver lifted their heads, to become aware of a dark-brown sludge that was raining down upon them.

'What the fuck! Where the hell did that come from?' asked the soldier crouching beside Pash.

Pash couldn't restrain a grin. 'Belgium.' And he peered from his sanctuary at the sight of scores of children scurrying across the road, regardless of safety. They hadn't seen chocolate for years.

The lieutenant led Pash and his men through the remains of the textile factory that had been taken over by the Kaiser Wilhelm Institute as the heart of the German atomic project. Nothing in the appearance of the place would have suggested how important the site had been. Artillery had punched massive holes through virtually every wall still standing. The roof had long gone and everywhere lay the remains of German technological pre-eminence, now just one more graveyard of Nazi ambition.

They paused in the courtyard to take in the scene. Walking up to join them was one of Pash's forward party, Guzzman, a child-like creature, too young for his uniform, completely out of place amongst the battle-weary soldiers. 'Colonel Pash.'

'Morning, Guzzman. What have we got?'

'Ah, the lieutenant –'

'Up there,' interrupted the lieutenant, indicating the heavens. Pash peered skywards. 'We picked them up two days ago, headed for France in the bus. Didn't know till yesterday who they were.'

There, suspended thirty feet above the ground,

from a mobile bridge-building crane, swung the bus in question. At the windows could be seen a dozen or more terrified faces: the atomic research scientists of the Kaiser Wilhelm Institute.

'I know it ain't exactly according to the Geneva Convention, but I was told to put them someplace safe.' Pash stared at the lieutenant in total incredulity. 'I'm a bridge-builder, Colonel, not a jailer.'

'Is Heisenberg up there?'

'No, but we've got him. He made his get-away on bicycle a couple of days ago and we picked him up at his home town. We also got Von Wizsacker and Hahn,' Guzzman said proudly, nodding towards the bus.

'Did you question them?'

'All day yesterday.'

'And?'

'It made my hair stand on end. They used slave labour and –'

'I've got the picture. Any hardware?'

'We found something that might be an isotope-separator and we also found a fairly primitive nuclear-pile, built into a cave over that way. Not much else yet.'

'Right. Let's get started.' The lieutenant made a signal and the bus slowly began its descent.

The Superchief was the pride of the Central Pacific Railways, a gleaming glass-and-aluminium diesel that streaked across the prairies towards Chicago. The dining car, resplendent with white linen tablecloths and wood-grained panelling, boasted the finest in Mid-western fare. Anything and everything was available, as long as it was steak. Groves, de Silva and Latrobe were midway through their meal. A conductor moved with dignity through his domain, until he was stopped by Groves's raised hand. The general wiped some gravy from his mouth. 'We're late. Leacock Crossing,' he said finally, looking up at the conductor.

'Pardon me, sir?'

'We passed it eight minutes late. We should have been there at 8.50, not 8.58.'

The conductor could only nod silently, eyes wide.

'Make sure you report it.' The general jerked his head towards the head of the train, indicating to the conductor that he was now dismissed. De Silva and Latrobe looked sideways at each other, but said nothing.

'I spent my childhood gazing at trains,' explained Groves. 'I liked the idea of them running all over the country, as regular as clockwork. About the only thing in my childhood that was.' Groves took a big bite of his steak sandwich, dripping gravy back on to his plate.

Latrobe lifted his coffee cup. 'Did I tell you Oppenheimer wants another twelve hundred people up at Los Alamos – 1,207, to be exact. Says he's going to resign if he doesn't get them.'

'He won't resign. You should keep off the black coffee, it destroys the stomach lining.' Another huge bite of steak, through which he mouthed, 'He's going for the implosion method. If it takes another 1,207 men to get it right, then he gets them.'

A sudden squeal from the wheels beneath them and then a violent wrench turned the gentility of the dining car into chaos. Plates flew, glasses crashed, the general's sandwich threw itself on to de Silva's impeccable uniform as Latrobe's coffee poured itself into his lap.

'What is this?' Groves got to his feet and peered through the window at the jet-black countryside.

Outside, the front engine of the Superchief was bearing down upon a motorcycle courier and a staff car parked by the tracks. Someone stood astride the tracks swinging a red lantern. The noise of the brakes reached a climax and then fell to a hiss of escaping hydraulics. The courier kicked his machine into life and sped up the track towards the rear of the train. De Silva and Latrobe leaned out of a window.

'General Groves?' yelled the courier. The two colonels nodded and signalled to him to come on board.

Inside, a furious general snatched the courier's pouch and removed from it a buff-coloured envelope marked ALSOS. TOP SECRET. EYES ONLY.

'This was flown into Weedburg Base a few hours ago. We wired through to have the train stopped here,' explained the courier. Groves shoved the envelope back into the pouch, looked up and down the car and nodded to Latrobe. 'I think I'd better read this somewhere safe.'

Latrobe followed him to the general's private compartment. Having locked the door behind them, Groves opened the door to the toilet, squeezed himself inside and shut the door behind him. Then he read:

> MOTHER HAD NO BABY - NOT EVEN PREGNANT - DOCTORS PRONOUNCED HER INFERTILE. MORE. B. PASH.

'Colonel.'

Latrobe opened the door. 'General?'

'Here.' He handed Latrobe the message. 'Put this in my safe, way in the back. It doesn't come out without my permission.'

'Sir, what is it? Should we really be suppressing this?'

'You tell me, Colonel.' Latrobe read the message. 'It's very delicate. You let any of my longhairs get a look at that, especially the Jewish prima donnas, and everything might come to a halt. Take Hitler out of the equation and they just might run out of stink. Why chance it?'

'But doesn't this change our priorities, sir? It means we're the only game in town.'

Groves levered himself up from the pan and locked himself eye to eye with the colonel. 'That's absolutely right, Colonel. There ain't nobody in sight of us now, and by my reckoning it's going to stay that way for the next twenty years. This is our moment in history. We have an opportunity to give this country the biggest stick in the playground.' For the first time Latrobe began to understand. They were no longer in a race to win a war. Groves had his eye on something much more permanent.

'Now, our Eggheads are going to hand it to us. But we've got a way to go yet. Let me tell you about those guys: don't let their airy notions fool you. They're just as ambitious as you and me; they taste success like everyone else. If we get them close enough, they'll go the whole way. But they aren't close enough yet.'

TEN

The winter snows still lay in heaps across the roofs of Los Alamos. The ground had turned into a brown sludge laced with the morning's frost. Oppenheimer and Serber had risen early to meet the morning bus from Santa Fe. The mud-streaked vehicle had just been cleared through the security gates and was turning slowly into its bay as they arrived. As the little welcoming party stepped up to the open door, Robert caught sight of a familiar face in the back of the bus and waved. Eventually the tall figure of George Kistiakowsky stepped down and was greeted warmly. 'Kisty', an affable, Russian-born explosives expert from the Harvard chemistry department, had recently become involved with Neddermeyer's experiments. But Oppenheimer was there to meet someone else. Kisty had brought a new boy with him, and this was who he beckoned to through the door. A slim, tweedy gentleman crowned with a mop of brown, wavy hair stepped down and extended his hand.

'Oppie,' said Kisty, 'this is James Tuck, from the British weapons research centre. James, this is Dr Oppenheimer and Dr Serber.' With the introductions completed, the four walked towards the accommodation section.

'I think you'll find a very friendly atmosphere here,' Oppenheimer began. 'Isolated, but that helps concentrate the mind. You'll be properly inducted later on. Did Kisty say anything about what you'll be working on?'

'He mentioned something about implosion.'

'Ah. Yes. But first there are one or two security precautions we have to take here. You'll soon get used to them.'

At the Security Centre new arrivals were interviewed by staff already familiar with the person's entire academic, professional and medical record. The centre controlled virtually all aspects of Los Alamos society – departures and arrivals, communications, even marital problems were dealt with. Inside the building was a row of small cubicles, into which the interviewee and interviewer entered from opposite sides. Shoenfield, a regular visitor to these little rooms, sat slumped in a chair amid a crowd of new arrivals. Babyface, perching on his shoulder, looked for amusement across the sea of drowsy faces. A voice called, 'Shoenfield, Booth Seven!' and he slid to his feet, casting a resigned look at his neighbour. Inside the booth he was confronted by a fierce looking WAC seated on the other side of the table.

'Dr Richard Shoenfield, ma'am. You wanted to see me?'

The WAC's massive bust heaved a sigh at the sight of Babyface and she pointed at the chair opposite. Spread out before her was a letter, which she took up and held in front of him. It was heavily scored with thick black lines.

'This letter cannot be sent. You have used the "B word" three times. You were requested not to use the "B word".'

'Can I tell you something? You're just the woman I wanted to see. What exactly is the "B word"?'

'It's censored.'

'I had a feeling it was. A friend of mine used the word censored.'

'Correct.'

'But I was then instructed not to use the word censored.'

'Correct.'

'How could I tell her not to use the word censored without using the word censored? Do you see what I mean?' He stared into her cold, lifeless eyes. 'No, I doubt that you do.'

The WAC laid the piece of paper on the table and folded her arms. In the distance a voice called, 'Klaus Fuchs, weekend pass, Booth Two.'

'Do you mind if I get a little personal for a second? How many times have I brought this letter to you guys?'

'I don't know.'

Shoenfield reached down and removed from his briefcase a sheaf of letters. 'OK, that's fair enough, you're a busy woman. I have the information right here.' He thumped the papers on the table in front of him. The good humour had vanished. 'Twenty-three times. How long does this go on?'

'Until you stop using that word.'

'OK. But I still don't understand.' He removed an earlier letter from the stack and showed it to her. 'See, I didn't use the "B word" in this letter, and yet you still censored it. Why?'

'Because, Dr Shoenfield, in that letter,' she said, nudging it as if it were a plague carrier, 'in that letter anyone reading it would understand that we censor letters.'

Shoenfield was incredulous. 'But that's why I wrote it!'

'That's why we censored it.'

Shoenfield thrust his arm across the table. 'Would you pinch me, please? Am I suffering delusions here or was I once a member of a great democracy?'

'I don't make the rules.'

'Well, sure as hell I don't make them. And Babyface, she doesn't, and you tell me you don't. So who does, for God's sake?'

The WAC sighed heavily again. Shoenfield realized that the meeting was over and got to his feet. 'No. No, sorry. Unfair question. If you gave me the answer, well, you know me, I'd probably put it in a letter and then you'd have to censor the damned thing.' In a rage he scooped up the letters, grabbed a hold of Babyface, charged out of the cubicle and tore past the bemused gaze of the new arrivals.

Out in the street Shoenfield swept on, head down, muttering dark incantations about the system. He didn't see Merriman and Kathleen coming in the opposite direction until he almost collided with them. Then all around him he saw the whole crazy world in which he now worked. Down the main street a pair of Sherman tanks were ploughing up the snow and mud. Riding on top of one of them were Neddermeyer and Parsons, treating everyone to hilarious mock victory salutes. On the pavement Merriman, loaded down with bags of shopping, tried to return the compliment.

Kathleen just stood there, enjoying the little piece of theatre.

'Hiya, Buttercup!'

'Hi, Richard.'

'Come to see the boys at play?' Shoenfield snapped to attention and gave his unique imitation of a salute as the parade swept by. 'Oh, by the way, I can't make the movies tonight. But I could join you both later for a beer, if you'd like that.' Shoenfield looked across at Merriman, who shifted his load uncomfortably. He could read the signals. 'Well, actually, I've just remembered that I promised to cut a rug with someone tonight. Don't like to break a date.' He winked at them both. 'What a day, eh?'

As soon as he was gone, Kathleen turned to Merriman. 'What's wrong with you?'

'Do you see much of him?'

'Yes, I like him.' Then, having caught his drift, she stopped and looked at him properly. 'Are you jealous?'

Merriman carried on a few paces, then he too stopped, and turned to her. He really didn't want to admit it, but, 'Yes.'

Kathleen laughed and Merriman felt his stomach tighten. She stepped up and took her parcels from him. 'Then you'd better do something about it.' She brushed his cheek with the lightest of kisses, and was gone.

Out at the testing site, the two tanks had been parked about thirty feet apart. They faced each other like a pair of giant beetles, either about to mate or do battle. Midway between them stood a large bulbous object, like a multi-faceted mine. To each facet was attached a wire, and these were gathered together and led across the sage-brush to a pair of sandbagged shelters. Inside one of the redoubts, surrounded by electronic monitoring equipment, Neddermeyer, James Tuck and Merriman were going through a series of last-minute checks.

Outside, Oppenheimer and Kistiakowsky were watching soldiers carrying high explosives from the munitions truck. Tuck emerged from the redoubt and caught a look of puzzlement on Oppenheimer's face. He pointed at a curious wedge-shaped piece of explosive headed towards the sphere.

Tuck explained. 'Think of these explosive wedges as forming a lens. They re-direct the shock waves, rather as a lens refracts and re-directs light towards a particular focus.'

'Focus.' Oppenheimer repeated the word with an air of revelation.

'We've used the idea at Porton Down, for our armour-piercing shells.'

As they made their way across the uneven ground they overtook two men with a stretcher carrying two of the wedges. Tuck's lecture was cut short when the man to the rear stepped into a hole and fell to one knee. For a moment everyone held their breath and watched as he pushed himself back up and carried on. At the sphere, Merriman began the delicate process of loading the explosives. Handling each one as if it were a piece of Meissen china, he gently slipped it into its predetermined position inside the sphere.

'If this works, we'll be back on schedule,' Oppenheimer thought aloud.

'No one has ever used high explosives as a precision instrument before,' fussed Kisty.

'I know, but it's so simple. It swings the shock waves from convex into concave.' Neddermeyer beamed like a child who had just solved a jigsaw puzzle. 'Some orange, huh, Oppie?'

'After the explosion, Neddermeyer.'

Neddermeyer had loaded the final wedge, given the thumbs up and an airtight hatch had been screwed into place. As the scientists marched back to the redoubts, a jeep pulled up and someone stepped out. No one noticed him as they entered the nerve centre. Merriman got the equipment up and running and as Parsons, Tuck and Kisty shunted slowly through their check-list, Oppenheimer was handed a thin envelope – 'Sorry to disturb you, sir.' Oppenheimer couldn't even remember his face after he was gone.

The tension in the room had begun to wind up as laughter and wisecracks punctuated the technical jargon. Oppenheimer absent-mindedly ripped open the envelope and scanned the two lines:

JEAN TATLOCK DEAD. COMMITTED SUICIDE AT HER APARTMENT. WEDNESDAY, 5 JAN.

Oppenheimer staggered against something, then steadied himself. All he could hear was the thump of his own pulse; the activity around him had vanished. Then someone announced, 'Zero minus ten,' and they were into a countdown. Around him everyone had something to do, but for Robert it seemed that all the activity had lost its meaning. He clutched at the periscope which had been focused on the sphere in the middle of the field and swung himself behind it. Tears filled his eyes, so he pressed his face hard against the instrument. He could see nothing. 'Eight, seven, six . . .' He wrenched himself forward in the seat. It was Jean. Jean's face outside, through the 'scope. 'Four, three . . .' Jean was out there in the field, staring back at him.

The explosion knocked him backwards. A deep, resonating boom rolled across the hills. The meter in front of Neddermeyer showed the magnetic waves contracting sharply. His face lit up and he let out a terrific howl which seemed to roll across the countryside along with the dying sound of the explosion.

'It squeezed! It squeezed! We've got a compression! We're on the way!' And they were out, Neddermeyer, Parsons, Merriman and Tuck, tumbling towards the sphere.

'Once we get the mixture right, we're home free!'

Behind them Oppenheimer followed, the scrap of paper clenched tightly in his fist.

News of Neddermeyer's success crackled through the establishment like summer lightning. But the euphoria was tinged with a curious emptiness, for there was no sign of Oppie to share it. In fact the entire project after such a terrific breakthrough seemed strangely rudderless and adrift.

Oppenheimer had collapsed – physically, mentally and emotionally. For a while he had taken to walking alone among the pine forests and then later he simply sat in the garden and refused to take any calls or to see anyone. As these things do, the world began closing in on the project. Groves had found himself besieged by requests from Congressional inquiries about the fantastic expenditure all coming in under the heading 'expediting war effort'. He had hoped he might be able to bring Congress around to his viewpoint by arranging to have a select number of senators and congressmen briefed about the project, but this hadn't completely succeeded. And worse was to come from his own colleagues at the Pentagon.

He had barricaded himself in his office one day and given orders not to be disturbed, when suddenly the door to Bronson's office crashed open. Groves had just about got to his feet when a large truck tyre rolled through the door. Close behind it came General Melrose H. Barry. As Barry clearly had Groves's undivided attention now, he closed the door.

'I tried damn hard to get through to you through official channels, so when I failed I decided to bring you my problem personally. This is what my men have been riding around on. Look at it, Dick, it's a bald tyre.' Groves sank back into his chair. If he was going to have to listen, he might as well be comfortable. 'I don't know what kind of fool hassle you've got yourself into, but I get angry when it cuts into my territory. I've got to shift supplies around this goddam country. I need trucks, and those goddam trucks need tyres. Now, Dick, when I hear my trucks ain't movin' because of a goddam tyre shortage, I get real mad. And when I hear you're the cause of it, I want to kill somebody.'

Groves waited for his moment and then spoke, oozing charm. 'I'd like to help, Melrose, but no dice. I've got a triple-A priority, straight from the White House. We really need this product.'

Barry leaned against Groves's desk. 'Then maybe you need to do something. You're getting a lot of people's backs up in Washington, and all over for that matter. And let me remind you of something.' He tapped the stars on his epaulette. 'I've got two of these things. I see only one on you. That's going to count when this war is over, and Dick, I hope you get my meaning, because a lot of people will be looking for your ass. It better be well covered.'

After Barry had gone, Groves tried once more to raise Oppenheimer on the phone. But before the connection had been made the side door opened and Latrobe slipped in, closing the door again quickly on further trouble.

'Sorry to barge in on you, General. I can't hold them off any longer.'

'Who?'

'Senate Appropriation Committee. Two representatives out there.'

'Tell 'em I'm not buying any. Tell 'em the White House said there'd be no accounting until after the war.' Groves pushed Latrobe back through the door and as he began to close it, Bronson appeared. Before he even opened his mouth, Groves swore: 'Damn it, Bronson!'

'Sir?'

Groves sighed. 'It's all about ass, Bronson. You either kick it or you lick it, but that's what it's about.'

'Yes, sir.'

Groves stopped at the door. 'I apologize for my language, Bronson.'

'That's OK, sir.'

'I'm out on a limb at the moment. If my prima

donnas don't come through, you're looking at a piece of dead meat.'

Groves stood silently on the back porch of Oppenheimer's house. Robert was seated with his back to the house in a garden chair, his legs covered with a blanket. He had found the last patch of sunlight at the foot of his garden, and he looked as though he might stay there forever. The gramophone in the living room was playing Gounod's *Faust*, and the music was drifting out of the house into the mountain air.

Kitty, now about six months pregnant, shuffled up beside Groves in the gloom of the back porch and emptied her martini.

'How is he?' he said softly.

'Nursing a guilty dick, no doubt.'

'I don't think it's necessary to be vulgar.'

'Nothing I could say could approach the vulgarity of what you are building in our backyard.'

Groves turned away from the garden and stepped deeper into the shadows. 'Well, vulgar or not, I need him to come through on this. He owes it to his country – and to himself.' He looked at her squarely. 'He's the best, and he should have whatever he wants.'

'Don't try to recruit me, General. You don't need any help from me. And don't give me your homily on being a good wife, because I've heard it before.'

The front door had opened and footsteps echoed down the corridor. The voices of Peter and his nurse called out, announcing they were home.

'I'm in back,' Kitty called out. Groves remained in the shadows while little Peter jumped out on to the porch and ran to hug his mother.

'How was school?'

'Great, Mom. I drew a picture of a plane, see?' Kitty cooed over the drawing and looked out across to her husband.

Peter took the picture back and bounced out on to the grass. 'Dad, see what I did . . .' But he brought himself to a halt, learning to restrain the impulse to share things with his father. Robert hardly ever took any notice of his son, even when he was in a good mood. Now, to Peter, his father was just a mute stranger at the breakfast table. Peter turned back and disappeared quietly into his part of the house.

Groves slipped out of the shadows and into the garden. As he passed by the window he paused and looked back into the gloom of the porch. 'Kid needs his dad.'

'We all need him,' she replied. Groves grunted.

'Mrs Oppenheimer?'

'Yes?'

'Why did you put up with her for so long?'

'Because he's the best there is and he should have whatever he wants.' Touché. 'I don't live very well alone. I think you know he's my fourth husband. We met just after he and Jean had broken up the first time and he told a friend of his then that I was another of the walking wounded. He was right. I need him. And we all have different ways of defending our territory.'

None of that made any sense to Groves. He shoved his hands into his pockets and slowly paced out the length of the garden. The music of *Faust* seemed somehow clearer the farther he got from the house, though its meaning was lost on the general. He took hold of a nearby wooden chair and placed it beside

Robert. They both stared out towards the sierra. Finally Groves spoke, with surprising tenderness.

'I'm sorry. I'm sorry that the news took so long to reach you.'

Oppenheimer sighed and allowed the very slightest shake of his head. Groves continued. 'It just got lost in the system. The censors –' He knew there was no point in trotting out the same old excuses. He tried something different. 'You know, you can't be responsible for keeping someone else alive. Not possible. Not even to be expected.'

'I'm sorry, General. I've decided I can't work on this any more. I don't want to and I don't need to. Germany's just about finished, it's only a matter of time. You and I both know they can't pull a project like this together.'

'Sure . . .'

'I don't want to hear your arguments any more. I know the war's not over until it's over, but nevertheless . . .'

'Look, Doctor . . .'

'I don't understand the situation, General. I don't know what you want any more. This whole project was never going to produce a weapon in time to win the war. You knew that, Congress now knows it – even your colleagues at the Pentagon know it. No one else on this earth has the resources to produce what we're producing. Do they?'

Groves's expression was a steely grey. He stared ahead like the bow of a battleship.

'I've got rats in my skull,' Oppenheimer said, with his head in his hands.

'When I feel like that, I get down on my knees and pray. That's what gives me conviction.'

'You don't understand.' And he was right, Groves didn't. 'I know we can build this thing now, I just can't remember why any more. I'm being asked to throw too many balls in the air at the same time.'

Groves got to his feet and looked down at the broken figure before him. 'You let this slip out of your hands – out of *our* hands – and you can take my word for it, somebody else will catch it, sooner than you think. Maybe not in five, maybe not in ten years. But someone else will catch it, eventually. And think about this, too. If you walked off this project, what would that do to the reputation of Dr J. Robert Oppenheimer?'

Oppenheimer felt a sudden chill through to his bones. The last few rays of sunlight were dying in the west. The garden was now deep in shadow.

'Doctor, get out of that chair. Whatever fire you need, please find it – wherever you can. But for God's sake, get out of that chair.'

ELEVEN

The first that anyone knew that Oppie might have recovered from his depression was when someone caught sight of him sauntering down to the old riding-school stables with Merriman. He hadn't spoken to anyone at the labs for more than a week, though some had heard that he'd started spending a great deal of time with the young man from Chicago. When word came to Tech A that Oppie was down at the stables, Goethe and Fermi dropped their papers and trotted down to the corral. Merriman and Oppie were saddling up like a pair of old cowhands and when anyone asked, they claimed they were going out to look for stray cattle – the neighbouring ranchers' animals often wandered on to the site, causing all kinds of problems.

'Edward was wondering if you'd be at the lodge today,' Fermi asked as Oppie swung himself into the saddle.

'Morning, Franz. Looks like it's going to be a good one.'

The sight of the two horsemen surrounded by scurrying Eggheads was of keen interest to security. They liked to keep a tab on 'their' guys. Movement around the site, except on official operations, was meant to be restricted. And they had not had any official notification of this 'operation'. They peered from their watch-tower down at the stables.

'What the fuck –?'

'What's the story?'

'I think one of 'em's the professor, but I'm not sure.' No one except security noticed, but Oppie and Merriman were wearing identical clothing. From a distance, they were indistinguishable. The two of them rode out of the corral, then Oppenheimer turned his horse to the north, the other 'Oppenheimer' turned west. It was a neat trick, thought the guys in the tower. 'I guess things are getting back to normal.'

Oppenheimer and Merriman rendezvoused near a fork that led up towards the distant mesa. They rode together past the pine forests to the edge of a bluff that overlooked their valley. They had found no cattle along the way.

'I used to vacation out here. Peaceful, huh?' mused Oppie.

They walked their horses along the edge until they were brought up short by a vista of purple hills and snow-topped mountains. The air, always so crisp, cut through their lungs.

Merriman found himself extraordinarily moved. 'You know, just a few miles closer to the sun – or a few miles further away – and there'd be none of this. Everything looks tough and rugged, when really it's so delicate. There'd just be a cloud of gas or a block of ice, and no one in existence to see it. Makes you think, huh?'

'Maybe there's a divine plan after all.' Oppenheimer

reined in his horse and led it in a circle around Merriman. Merriman looked at him closely and saw how he had changed. He seemed an older man; tired, yet with a hard glint of determination. The boyishness was gone and in its place there was a note of cynicism in his words. '*Odi et amo* . . . I hate and I love – Catullus. Do you know it?' Merriman shook his head.

'I hate and I love. Why, you ask. Well, I don't know, but I do feel both. *Sentio excrucior* – and I feel agony.' He looked across at Merriman, almost pleading. 'Everyone wants to feel complete, Michael. When they don't or can't, that's when they feel destructive.' He followed that, oddly, with a harsh stinging laugh – not at Merriman it seemed, but at himself.

'General Groves would have us banish that kind of thinking. Maybe he's right.' Oppenheimer wiped the cold sweat from his face. The wind from the mesa was now chilling them both and the cattle had long been forgotten.

'Michael, we've got to test critical mass. I've watched you working, you've got good physical coordination. We could use you. Are you interested?'

'Yes.'

Oppenheimer turned his horse away from the view and nodded his head in the direction ahead. 'Good. Let me show you something.'

Omega Canyon was the name given to the laboratory established for some of the most dangerous experiments with radioactive material. Louis Slotin, an easy going Canadian physicist, Cyril Smith, a metallurgist, Kisty and Otto Frisch, a mathematical wizard from Germany who led the Critical Assemblies team, worked with the first real quantities of sub-critical material. Frisch welcomed them both as they came into the main laboratory.

'So you've come to see our toys, Michael. This is where we "tickle the dragon's tail".'

Before them was an apparatus supporting a stack of highly polished metal bricks. Each brick was about four inches square and a foot long. They were assembled to create a shallow cavity through which ran a narrow track. In the heart of the cavity were smaller, equally shiny bricks, about an inch cubed. These were made from Uranium 235.

'We build these up around the track – until we've almost reached sub-critical mass. But the point of the experiment is to determine how much of this stuff is needed to go "critical".' He moved his hand towards a slug of wine-coloured material – uranium hydride, about two inches by six. 'The slug of uranium is pulled by this weight. It begins here,' Frisch indicated the top end of the track, 'then accelerates at 32 feet per second. It passes between these uranium bricks . . . and we have an instant of critical mass. For a split second we have a chain-reaction. A momentary bomb. In the gadget, the slug will be moved into contact with the uranium outer mass and be kept there. Here it passes through very quickly.'

Oppenheimer leaned closer to the apparatus to admire its beauty. Despite the risks involved, he loved to visit the place and sit and talk with these people. 'Sometimes,' he said, 'these guys generate nearly 20 million watts of energy with this thing. It's as close as we can get to an atomic explosion.'

'Without blowing up,' Frisch added.

'Exactly,' Oppenheimer agreed. 'It is essential to determine precisely the amount of material the device is going to need.'

Frisch was clearly delighted with his toy. He beamed away as his visitors stood and admired it. 'Ten years ago I could hardly imagine the stuff. Ha! Only ten years!'

During that first week of May 1945, rumours bounced around Los Alamos like glow-worms in a bottle. Each scrap of new information was pulled apart, relished and passed on. As the weekend approached, anticipation was so high that some found it difficult to concentrate and work ceased on a range of projects. For the Hungarian-, German-, Italian- and Russian-born population the day they had hoped and prayed for since 1939 was at hand. With every up-date of the situation they hugged and kissed each other, while some wept with excitement.

During that same week Kitty had been preparing herself for the birth of their second child. She swayed from room to room, 'like a carnival float' she claimed, listening to the news on the radio. With every fresh report she seemed, curiously, more detached. Having shaken off his torpor, Robert had buried himself even more deeply in his work and now she seemed more alone than ever. Occasionally she was visited by some of the other wives, those she hadn't alienated with her heavy drinking and plain-speaking. 'Christ, it's like trying to walk with a grapefruit in your panties,' she complained. On 8 May she was driven to the hospital by her neighbour and was quickly admitted to the labour ward.

On 9 May the men were all summoned to the Fuller Lodge to hear the news – officially. Gathered round the radio were Oppenheimer, Fermi, Teller and Merriman, and behind them almost everyone else who could manage to squeeze into the room.

The announcer delivered the news to a respectful hush.

> I HAVE THE RARE PRIVILEGE OF SPEAKING FOR A VICTORIOUS ARMY OF ALMOST 5 MILLION MEN. THEY, AND THE WOMEN WHO HAVE SO ABLY ASSISTED THEM, CONSTITUTE THE ALLIED EXPEDITIONARY FORCE THAT HAS LIBERATED WESTERN EUROPE.

From the back of the room an almighty howl echoed to the wooden rafters and appeals for quiet punctuated the pause.

> THEY HAVE DESTROYED OR CAPTURED ENEMY ARMIES TOTALLING MORE THAN OUR STRENGTH.

Outside the same news was echoing across the rooftops from speakers dotted around the site. Doors were flung open and dozens of people rushed down into the streets. Vehicles were halted and commandeered, and their horns, from one end of the site to the other, built in a deafening crescendo.

> THEY HAVE SWEPT TRIUMPHANTLY FORWARD OVER THE HUNDREDS OF MILES SEPARATING CHERBOURG FROM LEIPZIG, LUBECH AND MUNICH.

No one wanted to be alone once they'd heard the

news. Feet thundered down corridors, lovers embraced, men and women wept openly.

In the hospital the news swept from room to room and resounded up from the street outside. Kitty held new-born Katherine to her breast as she smeared the tears from her own cheeks.

> THESE STARTLING SUCCESSES HAVE NOT BEEN BOUGHT WITHOUT SORROW AND SUFFERING. IN THIS THEATRE ALONE, 30,000 AMERICANS AND A COMPARABLE NUMBER OF ALLIES HAVE HAD THEIR LIVES CUT SHORT SO THAT THE REST OF US MIGHT LIVE IN THE SUNLIGHT OF FREEDOM.

'Has your husband been in to see you yet?' a nurse asked.

'He'll be along shortly. He's – you know . . .'

Back at the Fuller Lodge, Oppenheimer hadn't shifted from the one spot. Around him men were slapping each other on the back, while he already seemed preoccupied with something else. Wasn't the job over with now? He fumbled with the idea and its consequences and wondered where to go from here. Behind him, Merriman had taken out a pencil and scratched a line in his diary. 'A great day – now what?' As he snapped the diary shut Oppenheimer glanced over his shoulder and they smiled at each other.

> BUT AT LAST THIS PART OF THE JOB IS DONE. NO MORE WILL THERE FLOW FROM THIS THEATRE TO THE UNITED STATES THOSE DOLEFUL LISTS OF DEATH AND LOSS.

In the hospital lab Shoenfield had been called to take

a look at some of the animals. The radio reached them even there as he opened the last of the cages and removed one of the rabbits. He laid it beside a row of the poor beasts, all covered with suppurating sores, their eyes opaque, their breathing erratic. Outside the window the streets were filled with joyous noise.

'Shut the window.'

Shoenfield watched the creatures writhing on the table. When the room was quiet he switched on the Geiger counter and passed it slowly over the rabbits. It crackled and clicked wildly – and the needle went straight to the top of the scale. 'What the fuck are we doing here?'

A week later, when they got round to celebrating officially, it was the biggest party anyone had ever seen. Shoenfield, Kathleen and Merriman grabbed some drinks and wandered out on to the balcony to watch the fireworks. Great silver fountains of light arched across the sky, flooding the streets. Down below, coloured lanterns had been strung through the trees, food had been laid out on trestle tables and everyone was out there loving it. Somewhere, hidden amongst the trees, a navy band blew Glenn Miller tunes, while a conga line snaked through the scene.

'What will we all do when it's over?' Kathleen wondered aloud.

Shoenfield took a pull from his bottle of scotch and felt it course through his bloodstream. 'Start another one. 'S why I'm here. I'm in a profession with great prospects.' Kathleen laughed, but he was half serious, even though he was drunk. 'Well, I'm not wrong. We are descended from a long and noble line of predators.'

'Richard, you are irrepressible.'

'Tha's 'cause when I was young I caught a strong dose of social irresponsibility. I've been a happy man ever since.' He slipped behind Merriman and Kathleen and embraced them both. 'Come on, let's go over to the Fuller and dance.' He stepped none too steadily across the floor and beckoned them to follow.

As the sky exploded with silver fire Kathleen moved closer to Merriman's shoulder.

'What did you write?'

'In my diary? Something Oppie said today . . . I don't know.'

'Well?'

'Oh, I was just wondering whether there's intelligence out there that isn't descended from a long and noble line of predators.'

His face shone with the lights in the sky, but Kathleen had been gazing at his mouth. 'I want to kiss you,' she told him. He was surprised how close her mouth was to his, though he'd dreamed of its taste for months.

Inside the lodge they'd gone crazy. The tables had been cleared to make way for the dancing, a country band had been thrown together by the Engineers and the likes of Fermi and Teller were being teased into attempting a square dance. On the floor, the experts were cutting a rug. Fancy dress was the order of the day: cowboys and Indians danced across the floor and, in the heart of it, wearing a chief's headdress, Oppenheimer swayed to the music. He carried a handful of drinks across to his table, where Kitty and the general sat looking on.

'I never got a chance to congratulate you, Mrs Oppenheimer.'

'Thank you, General.'

'Professor!' Oppenheimer looked across as the general raised his bottle of seltzer.

'General?'

'To your little girl!'

Oppenheimer smiled and raised his glass too.

'What are you going to call her?'

'Katherine,' said Kitty. She looked across at her husband, but his gaze was across the floor. He had barely bothered to look at the child since Kitty had returned from the hospital two days before. 'But we've already nicknamed her Toni.'

From out of the crowd an MP stepped forward and nodded to the general. Then he tapped Oppenheimer on the shoulder and leaned towards him. 'Sir, is it true that now we've KO'd Germany, we're all going home from here?' Oppenheimer flashed a look at the general, but said nothing.

'I'll drink to that,' said Kitty.

Suddenly Oppenheimer entered into the spirit of things. 'Now just a moment everybody.' 'Geronimo' swept on to the dance floor, his hands held high. 'Just a moment now. It seems there's a shortage of partners here.' He dropped his hand to his heart and went on in mock seriousness: 'So, by way of a thank you from the longhairs to the military for their sterling efforts overseas . . .' He eyed his prey, seated innocently at the table sucking on a bottle of seltzer, 'a warrior dance!'

Oppenheimer wrenched Groves to his feet and began to propel him about in a death-defying polka across the quickly cleared floor. The band caught on immediately while the audience shrieked and whooped in amazement. Eventually these two spirits of the dance paused in a tangle of limbs. But then, to Oppenheimer's amazement, Groves shouted: 'You follow, I'll lead!' And the pair whisked around the circle of faces like a Catherine wheel, accompanied by a wild, rhythmic clap.

From outside the music was reduced to a regular boom, boom, boom of crashing boots on the wooden floor. Michael and Kathleen had strolled away from the noise and people, looking for somewhere they could share together. He talked about his brother in the Philippines, the one the family was so proud of. He talked of the two kids he'd been at high school with who had been blown away at Guadalcanal, and how their deaths had changed the war for him and made him want to leave the university and join up, right then and there. And he talked about the guilt he felt, being so cut off from his family.

They stopped somewhere, he couldn't remember where afterwards.

'I want to kiss you again.' Kathleen reached up and took his head in her hands and opened her mouth to him. She held him to her as though she'd always meant it.

'I notice some of you dancing close together. I don't like the look of it.'

It was way past midnight back at Fuller Lodge. The band-leader had broken it up at the end of a bar and signalled a roll on the drums. Those who had stayed were now being treated to a wonderful floor-show. Up on the stage, his hands wrapped round the microphone, Shoenfield was presenting a once-in-a-lifetime impersonation of the general – who had retired from the scene an hour before.

'There are bosoms here, and that could lead to pregnancy. And there are too many men in this camp getting hard-ons after sunset. Now, any guys who get outta hand, or in hand, after that time will havta turn their peckers over to the FBI for . . . for . . .'

But he never managed to finish. From on top of a ladder, high in the rafters, someone emptied a bucket of water on the 'general'.

The explosion of laughter travelled across to the Admin. Block, where the real general was burning the midnight oil. He'd been sitting in the dark waiting for a long-distance phone call. When the bell suddenly jangled, he jumped at the receiver.

'Hallo? Yeah, that's great. That's great. What? No it is not over. I don't want Pash back here, no. Tell him to make for Stassfurt. If we don't the Russians will, and there's God knows how much uranium over there. Tell Pash I want it here. And listen, there's too many of those goddam German rocket scientists running about. I know that, but I want them grabbed and kept in our zones.' Groves glanced up from his desk to the sight of a Red Indian standing in his doorway. Oppenheimer was slouched against the door frame. 'OK. Listen, I'll call you back.'

He hung up, shoved a pack of cigarettes towards Oppenheimer and listened to the faint sounds drifting across from Fuller Lodge.

'They're having a great time, eh?' Groves beamed.

Oppenheimer removed the headdress and slumped into the chair on the other side of the desk. He took a cigarette and lit it. 'Sure. They think it's all over.'

'Over?' Groves leaned across to a beautifully made model of the uranium bomb on his desk. 'Over?' he repeated. He ran his finger across its shell. 'In Europe, OK. But what are the Japanese doing, shooting squirrels?'

'No, they're not shooting squirrels. But that's not the issue. The Japs don't have the technology. They're not capable.' The two were intent on the object before them. 'They're not going to threaten us with one of these things, so why do we need it? Why are we going ahead with all this?'

Groves tapped the end of the model and sent a little 'bullet' sliding into the 'uranium core'. 'Sweet, isn't it?' He surveyed Oppie benignly, then raised himself to his feet. 'Come and take a look at something with me.'

Groves and Oppenheimer walked together in silence, down the street towards the ordnance shop. They slipped quietly through the deserted corridors to the hangar at the back. Street lights filtered through frosted-glass windows and spilled across the floor. They were alone. Groves stepped up to the two enormous vessels, suspended from an overhead crane. One had 'Fat Man' chalked across its huge steel barrel designed to carry the plutonium bomb. The other was 'Little Boy', longer and narrower in shape, ready for the uranium bomb. For now they were just empty casements, easing back and forth on their lines.

'What we have here is nothing. These steel drums have the potential of being the most expensive containers of nothing in the entire world.'

'But the theory is there now, it's established. Virtually proven.'

'Then make them work!' Groves countered. '*Then* you'll have something! An irresistible something.'

'You mean a threat.'

'Maybe – but it's our threat.'

Oppenheimer looked hard at the general. 'A threat to whom?'

Groves ignored the question. 'You know, sometimes I wonder – are we working on them or are they working on us?' Then he looked back at his man. 'Give 'em dignity, Doctor. Then the world will know what you can do – and what they mean.'

Oppenheimer stared up at the empty casements. 'When I first started thinking about this, I reminded myself that I was a Jew, that I had a responsibility to help defeat the evil that had raised its head in Europe. The monster is dead now. The question remains: were my motives ever the same as yours?'

'Sure they were. They still are.'

'I know what you want, General, and I don't mind admitting – it frightens me.'

By two in the morning Fuller Lodge was littered with the remnants of the party. Mostly these were people in crumpled heaps, sprawled across sofas and armchairs. Others had got down to their regular game of poker, while a few picked themselves up and shuffled towards the door. Merriman and Kathleen had snuggled up together on a sofa, watching Shoenfield taking bets. Merriman had little idea of what was going on, except that Shoenfield kept nodding in his direction.

The bets made, Shoenfield grabbed a banana from a bowl of fruit and tossed it at Merriman, who sat up just in time to catch it. 'M'boy, you have been selected for a mission of outstanding importance. Welcome aboard.' Shoenfield advanced, his hand outstretched. He hauled Merriman to his feet and threw his arm around his shoulder. Merriman stood to attention, shouldering the banana, which Babyface then plucked from his grasp. 'Farewell, Kathleen, I've always loved you dearly,' swooned Shoenfield. Then he forced an 'about turn' and the two men marched out to cries of 'You'll never make it!'

Outside the Admin. Block Shoenfield waited across from the guard house for the operation to begin. Merriman had slumped his head to Shoenfield's shoulder and couldn't have cared less. The phone rang in the guard house, and the sentry crossed to the office to answer it. Shoenfield hugged himself with delight. 'That's the guys up at Fuller, come on.' They slipped past and up the steps to the entrance. Inside, they waited while their eyes got used to the light. Merriman had just begun to look about. Suddenly, he realized where they were.

'Richard, you're crazy! They'll kill us if they find us here.'

'A bet's a bet.'

'What bet?'

'One hundred bucks says I can stick a banana in the general's safe.' Shoenfield tried to stifle his laughter but couldn't control it. 'It'll kill him!'

'Are you out of your mind?'

But Shoenfield had already started down the corridor, Babyface tagging quietly along behind. At the door to Groves's office Shoenfield pulled out a set of keys and flipped through them for the most likely choice. Merriman took hold of the knob and gave it a twist.

'It's unlocked.'

'Damn, I wanted to break in.'

They crept across to the huge safe, sitting snugly in an alcove. Shoenfield tossed a torch at Merriman and fished a long roll of paper from his pocket. 'Shove the light on.' He looked at his list of numbers, seemingly about a yard long.

'Jesus, how much time will this take?'

'I hope only a couple of minutes.' He hunched himself up against the box and took hold of the combination dial. 'I got Feynman to figure it out on the IBM machine. If they can calculate for the gadget, they can devour this little baby.' Then to his great surprise he got his first hard click. He checked his figures again and got the last two tumblers into place. The crank lock slid up and the door swung slowly open. The torch scooped across stacks of TOP SECRET files and then into Merriman's panic-stricken face.

'All right. Shove your banana in and let's get out of here.'

'You've got it.'

'No, I haven't.'

'Michael, I threw it at you.'

'No, you didn't. Oh, yes you did.'

'So what the fuck have you done with it?' Merriman looked over his shoulder at Babyface. 'She's eaten the fuckin' thing!' Babyface tossed the empty skin across the floor and grinned at them.

'Oh God. Come on, Richard, let's just get out of here.'

Richard wrenched a flask from his hip pocket and

took a swig. 'We'll have to think of something else to stick in there.'

'The banana skin!' Merriman crawled towards it on his hands and knees.

Shoenfield moved the torch beam back into the safe and caught sight of a file at the top of the stack: 'Plutonium Tests: Oak Ridge', he read under his breath. 'Jesus . . .'

'I can't find the fuckin' thing,' Merriman hissed.

Shoenfield opened the file and scanned through it. Something he saw took him by the throat and squeezed the booze straight out of his veins. He let the thing drop and stared at some horrible vision that had been conjured up in his imagination.

'Come on, let's just get out of here.' Merriman took the file, shoved it back in the safe and closed the door.

TWELVE

He called the site Trinity. He said he'd been reading John Donne at the time.

> Batter my heart, three person'd God; for, you
> As yet but knock, breathe, shine, and seek to mend;
> That I may rise, and stand, o'erthrow me, and bend
> Your force, to break, blow, burn, and make me new.

His allusion to taking control of a divine power to break, blow and burn was one he kept to himself for the moment. Anyway, it was a piece of territory, some 200 miles south down Route 85, past Albuquerque and San Antonio. Close to the Alamogordo Air Base, it lay in lonely desert country midway between the towns of Carrizozo and Truth or Consequences. Flat as a pancake, it stretched, treeless, in every direction, for more than twenty miles. The region was known to the Spanish conquistadors as Journada del Muerto (Journey of Death) because so many had perished trying to cross it. Here they planned to detonate the first atomic device. It couldn't really be called a bomb; it wouldn't be fired from a cannon, dropped from an aircraft or detonated in the conventional sense. Even if it worked, and they didn't know whether it would, it was still a 'device'.

It was June, the sun was high and the land had begun to bake. Rising out of the sage brush a hundred-foot steel tower stood sentry over the desert. In its shadow, a curious scene of contradictions was taking place.

'What's going on?' Wilson emerged from his tent and watched a line of cattle amble across in front of him. The local ranchers had grazed their animals on this ground for generations, and they saw no reason why they should stop now. But the US Army had other ideas. The ranchers were invited to sell up their properties, but they'd refused. Then the army asked them to round up their strays, but that proved a waste of time too because the cattle kept wandering back on to the land, where the windmills pumped up water from the ground. So the army dealt with that by shooting all the water-tanks full of holes. Still the animals refused to leave. Finally the army decided to round the cattle up themselves.

'Oppie, what's happening?' Oppenheimer looked up from a drafting table set beneath the tower and peered through the glare at workmen riveting steel joists into place. 'Oppie?'

'We're still working on the fallout radius.' He tapped the blueprint in front of him, his finger hitting the centre of a set of concentric circles.

'No, there.' Wilson pointed at the cattle being herded together by a fleet of jeeps.

'Well, what does it look like?' Several Army Engineers, standing in the back of their jeeps, were firing sub-machine guns into the air. The cattle stumbled first one way, then the other. The wheels churned up the dust and hoofs trampled across the maze of thick black cables that had been fed out to the tower. Oppenheimer gathered up his drawings and walked through the dust to the tent. 'Can't see a damn thing out there.'

Deke Parsons stepped over to where Wilson stood, and whistled to a party of workmen nearby: 'Get the fuckin' cables behind them.' Parsons watched as the dust began to settle. Then, suddenly, they all heard the cold, ratchet sound of weapons being reloaded and cocked. Shots rang out and, one by one, the cattle fell to their knees.

'What are they doing?' screamed Wilson.

'Rangers wouldn't move them. I guess the army stopped negotiating,' said Parsons. The shots continued, more cattle fell and around them men put down their tools to stand and watch. Up in the tower they wiped their foreheads and pointed at the dead beasts. Faces appeared at the entrances to the tents, unable to believe what they saw.

'This has gone too far,' said Wilson, almost to himself.

'They tore up a whole run of ground cable. Ruined two days' work.'

'No, I mean the whole project's out of control.' Wilson turned to Oppenheimer and saw that he was still hunched over the same blueprint. The gunfire had ceased and all that remained was a chilling silence.

Then, finally, Oppenheimer spoke: 'Edward, this estimate seems low compared to last week's figures.'

Teller was completely thrown by Oppenheimer's single-mindedness: he seemed to be completely unaware of what had just happened. He tried: 'But those figures didn't reflect fast neutron fission in the tamper . . .' but he dried up before he could finish.

'Jesus,' sighed Wilson, 'all we're thinking about here is getting to the end. Rush, push on, speed, deadlines . . . Oppie, look at that fuckin' thing.' He jerked his thumb at the tower. 'No one's thinking about consequences!'

'Can it, Wilson. About ten minutes ago I threw you a calculation. When am I going to get the answer . . .?'

'He's right, Oppie. I think we need to talk over some of the things we've been thinking about.'

'That sounds a bit mysterious, Edward.'

'It's no secret. Look, the thing is becoming something real. Soon someone's going to decide to use it. It's going to affect lives. I'm talking about *people*, you know. Oppie, I think we need to talk.'

Oppenheimer was startled by the outburst of feeling. He was angered by it, too. Angered, because the priorities seemed so clear – and yet, had he really cut himself off from all those feelings? He looked across the field of dead and dying cattle. What had happened to him? How could he not have noticed? 'OK.' He looked across the men standing round him. 'Tonight, at my place.'

That afternoon Wilson took a drive across to the Omega Lab. As he rode the jeep up and down over the contours of the land, he felt his pulse quickening. It was all rushing along too quickly. He'd seen it happen before on other large projects. The closer you got to the pay-off, the faster it went, the more mistakes you made. Ever since May, it seemed, ever since the German surrender the pace had quickened, the pressure increased. Why? What was the race? All Wilson could think was – where were they going?

He slipped into the lab complex and searched out Merriman. He was pointed towards the main control lab where Merriman and his colleagues were gathered round the stack of U235 bricks. Wilson edged towards Michael's shoulder. 'How's it going?'

'We're getting there.'

Merriman was tickling the dragon. At one end of the track was a slug of plum-coloured uranium. Suspended from it was a wire leading to a weight. Halfway down the slide was the stack of U235 bricks. The needle on the Geiger counter was dancing back and forth. Merriman readjusted some controls, waited for the background reading to settle and then nodded to his colleague.

'Watch this.'

His colleague removed a simple screwdriver that had been holding back the slug and it slipped forward. The counter went berserk, the needle jumped off the scale and the U235 bricks glowed blue-white. For that fraction of a second, everything had gone critical.

'OK, let's have the calibrations as quickly as possible.'

Wilson put a hand on his shoulder. 'Can you give me a minute?' Merriman looked up and smiled.

The two of them strolled together down the drive, towards the main gate. Wilson didn't say a word until they were past the gate and embraced by the expanse of the mesa.

'You going to Oak Ridge?'

'Yes. Frisch can't pick up the slugs. I said I'd go.'

'Can you go via Chicago?'

'Why?'

'There's something there I want you to bring back.' An afternoon breeze just lifted the collars of their shirts. Merriman looked across at Wilson, who preferred to stare straight ahead. 'A lot of the guys in Chicago – you know, Szilard, Ralph Lapp, about twenty guys – they're proposing a petition. They're saying they're opposed on moral grounds to the use of the device. Szilard wrote to the White House back in March, got nowhere. Now they say they're more concerned than ever.'

Merriman kicked up some dust with his boot. 'So am I. I've got a brother in the Philippines . . .'

'Look, Michael, we just want to get it discussed. We should at least know what it says. I hear they might send it to the president.'

Merriman nodded. 'I could spend a day in Chicago.' He left Wilson at the gate and walked back to the lab. 'To the president . . .' he thought to himself. 'These guys!'

Oppenheimer was nervous about having the discussion at his house, and that didn't make sense to him. As he sat in the living room, waiting for the first to arrive, he thought how just a couple of years ago he'd have been out there ringing doorbells, getting people to meetings, stirring up their consciences. Now he had the jitters about a meeting with a couple of friends. He felt waves of anxiety about the project, about his relationship with Groves, about his relationships with everyone on the project – what would happen once it was all over.

He didn't stir from his chair while the children

were having supper, nor when they were put to bed. He was in the same place when the first guests arrived. Their conversation washed over him as Kitty poured the drinks. Then, each in their turn, they filed up to see the new baby cradled in the arms of the Indian nurse. Oppenheimer nodded to them all as they returned to the living room and gathered round. They nibbled at the subject for an hour or so, but he hardly said a word.

He looked hard at Wilson and wondered who the man really was. He kept talking about murder. 'You wouldn't recognize a moral argument if it jumped up and bit you. How can you rationalize pre-meditated murder?' Wilson said to Johnny Mount, one of the guys from Princeton.

'He's such a boy,' mocked Teller.

'Bullshit!' Mount could take care of himself. 'What are you talking about? Pre-meditated murder? This is war. It's about winning.'

'But at what cost? I mean, what principles are we fighting to protect?'

'We fire-bombed Hamburg, Dresden, Frankfurt. How many Krauts died then? I didn't hear anyone squealing about that.'

Kitty had retreated to the children's room. This kind of talk distressed her deeply. Although she gave the appearance of being a tough cookie, she actually found talk of war and mass-destruction, whoever the victims, deeply upsetting. As she watched the nurse putting the baby down for the night, Wilson's harangue filtered along the corridor.

'What are you saying, that as there's a sliding scale of horror, so there's a sliding scale of responsibility?

We have no idea what we're unleashing here. We haven't even talked about radiation poisoning. Has anybody even looked at long-term effects?'

'For God's sake, divorce physics from morality,' somebody suggested.

Oppenheimer stared at the faces around him. He was genuinely amazed, and a little intimidated, by the depth of feeling in the room. Teller wanted to know how anyone could simply outlaw a weapon – even a theoretical one. Wilson talked about poison gas and how that had been successfully banned, but no one had any faith in anyone doing the same for this weapon – something that was, potentially, omnipotent. What about the newly created United Nations? Just another version of the old League of Nations, and what had that done to prevent mass destruction of civilians?

Wilson appealed to his boss. 'Oppie, you've got to speak for those among us with a conscience. We must have a voice in the decision.'

'Yeah, and speak on behalf of those kids sheltering in foxholes at this moment. I know what they'd say. Japan has only itself to blame.'

'I wouldn't give a shit if the whole goddam place went up in smoke,' broke in Mount.

'I am thinking of the consequences. It's not just the extermination of thousands of Japanese, it's what it does for all of us afterwards. The potential scale of war – it's just too unimaginable. What if they drop a bomb on Chicago?'

'Afterwards is afterwards. Let's get it over with now.'

Oppenheimer heard the clock in the hall begin to chime and he glanced at his watch. 'Excuse me for a moment, gentlemen.' He levered himself out of his chair and headed down the corridor towards the bathroom. Kitty caught him as she came out of Peter's room.

'Peter asked if you'd take him riding tomorrow. It's Saturday.'

'I can't.' She hushed him with a finger to her lips, then closed the door and walked with him to the end of the corridor. Oppenheimer leaned against the bathroom door. 'I just can't,' he whispered. 'Why can't you take him?'

Kitty opened the door to the nursery. 'Come and look at Toni. She's so beautiful.' She looked down at the sleeping baby and ran her fingertips across the crown of the child's head.

When she looked up to Robert, there was just the open door to the bathroom and the sound of running water. Then he called out: 'Listen, Kitty, you might want to go and have supper at the lodge. I'm . . . I'm . . .'

'Goodnight, darling,' she whispered to Toni.

Robert appeared at the bathroom door.

'How long are they going to be?' she asked.

He rolled his eyes to the ceiling and shook his head. 'It could take all night. I don't know.'

'You look exhausted, Robert.' But he had already stepped back into the corridor. She sat down beside the crib and listened to the angry men.

'It really is Pandora's box, if you think about it. I mean it. We have no idea what could follow.'

'What you guys are really talking about is expediency.'

'Hold it, hold it.' Neddermeyer had had enough.

'Oppie, we need some guidance, we're going around in circles.' Oppenheimer dragged his fingers through his hair and collapsed into his chair again.

'I don't know. Look, gentlemen, I appreciate we have a lot of strong feelings here,' they clung to his words, 'and I promise you, I will find the appropriate moment to express them. I think, probably, the best thing now is if we try and summarize the discussion. I'll take some notes and then perhaps we'd better call it an evening.'

When Kitty tiptoed into the study at about two in the morning, Robert was hunched over his desk, fast asleep. Around his feet lay the screwed-up pages from his notepad, strewn about like snowballs. She picked up one and unrolled it under the light. He'd drawn up two columns, one headed 'Pros', the other 'Cons'. In each were dozens of scribbled notes, but no conclusion.

'What time is it?' He was awake. 'Oh God, I can't sleep without dreaming about it. I can't let it go.'

Kitty needed an answer. 'You're not thinking of resigning, are you?'

He sighed. 'No. I'd be written off as a failure. It's too late, no one would understand. Especially not in this climate.' He dropped his head into his hands and leaned back in the chair. His body ached all over and all he wanted was endless sleep. He dragged his hands across his face again and gathered together the papers on his desk. His thoughts went back to Groves that day in the garden, and the general's words echoed in his head: 'If you let this slip, somebody else will catch it. What would that do to the reputation of Dr J. Robert Oppenheimer?' He went on in a stronger voice:

'We've put too much into this, Kitty. Our success depends on its success. We're all concentrating on one point – and I have to agree with it. We must make the damned thing. But what's beyond it . . .' She wound her arm around his shoulders and kissed his head. 'On the bright side, there's a possibility of a remarkable, limitless source of energy, constantly renewable. It's a fantastic step forward, almost beyond imagination. The energy that created the universe – and I will have tamed it. You know what I said before, "technically sweet"? That's it.' Robert reached up and pulled his wife down on to his lap. They sat there holding each other and enjoying the embrace, the familiar smells, the warmth.

'God, I need to talk to you. Sometimes I don't know where you are,' she said.

They remained there, comfortable in each other's arms – and would have stayed there all night, but 'Jesus, I'd forgotten!' Kitty was tipped out of the chair and he was on his feet.

'What?'

'I've got to rush. I haven't even packed.'

'Packed?'

'Washington! Goddam it! Groves and I are flying out at six o'clock. It's supposed to be a big deal. We might even meet with the president.' He was already in the hall – and the rest of it would just have to wait.

THIRTEEN

Washington in June is like a sauna. By day, the air hangs like a suffocating cloud and by night, the cicadas in the swamps send up a constant shrill note. From June until September, the business of government grinds to a halt and the place is deserted. It is, after all, a one-industry town. But the summer of 1945 was different. The business of government carried on while the war was still there to be fought. There was a new president; a man who liked poker, bourbon and straight talking – or so they said. No one knew much else about him, and most people didn't care. They were still mourning the man who'd been in the White House since the beginning of 1933.

While America waited with growing impatience for the war with Japan to end, in Washington they were steeling themselves for one of the most critical decisions any government had taken in modern times. Carefully selected individuals, from military strategists to scientists, had been summoned to report to a committee that was being convened at the Pentagon. The Interim Committee had been charged with advising the president on the use and control of the S–1 –

what the inhabitants at Los Alamos called the 'gadget': the atomic bomb.

Groves had already briefed the new president, Harry Truman, about the work they were doing out in New Mexico. Truman seemed to have been impressed, though he later admitted that he hadn't understood a word of it. After Groves had finished his 'show-and-tell' routine, the Secretary of War, old 'Colonel' Stimson, briefed Truman on the diplomatic angle – in particular how the bomb would affect relations with the Soviets. No one was certain whether any of what he said had sunk in either. The one subject they did not discuss was whether or not the thing should ever be used. That's why they had set up the committee, and Groves and his boy wonder would be the star witnesses. When Groves next went to Los Alamos, he told his colleagues Truman had been like a little boy on a toboggan. The committee would be a piece of cake.

Oppenheimer watched the boats on the Potomac from the back seat of Groves's Buick. Seated beside him, Groves's eyes were fixed on the road ahead. This whole exercise, so far as he was concerned, was an opportunity for bureaucratic belly-aching. He just wanted to get it over with. For the man next to him, though, it was a nightmare. He was carrying the collective consciences of the entire scientific community. Although Fermi and other scientists would be there, as project leader they would all be looking to him for a lead. Trouble was, instead of being at the head of a great project, charging towards its goal, he felt everyone pulling in separate directions. The whole thing was coming apart.

They passed the Jefferson Memorial and took the exit for the Pentagon. Groves checked his watch. They were early. 'We've got time to stop off at Carlucci's for coffee and doughnuts.'

'This could all unravel. We're losing focus. Running out of steam . . .'

Groves took a long hard look at Oppenheimer. He sat crumpled up like a blanket in the back of the car. Groves searched, but couldn't see the arrogant young man he'd met out at the airfield near Livermore – three years ago, was it? The general realized that if he was to get what he wanted from Oppenheimer, he was going to have to do some quick work.

'Bronson, pull over.' Bronson slowed the car down and brought it to a halt in the middle of nowhere. Just a piece of Washington freeway, surrounded by grass and trees, somewhere up near the Pentagon. 'Now, go take a leak or something.'

'Sir, this is a public park.'

'Then admire the flowers. I want to do some shouting.'

Oppenheimer heaved a sigh and collapsed further into the seat. After Bronson had gone each waited for the other to speak.

'Look,' Oppenheimer finally started, 'I agreed to listen to everyone's thoughts on this thing. There are some pretty hard feelings about what we're doing.'

Groves let him run on.

'Since Germany surrendered, the objectives don't seem too clear to many people. A lot of them think we should stop the whole project.'

'Free discussion!' Groves came down like an axe on dry kindling, seizing his opportunity. 'Filling their heads with information they didn't need, information they shouldn't have had. They're rattled! What did they think we were doing?' Oppenheimer couldn't respond. 'Listen, you tell them about Okinawa. The gooks lined themselves up and blew themselves to pieces rather than surrender. Twelve thousand Americans died on Okinawa – *twelve* thousand! How can they sit around polishing their consciences when we could put an end to all of it with one big bang?'

'Ah, but will it stop there?'

'Look, Doctor.' Groves rubbed his chin and chewed his words over for a moment. 'You're one of the most intelligent men I've ever met. I'm not stupid either. I know I can't tell you that you can't have a crisis of conscience – but I can ask you whether it's going to prevent you being an effective leader, whether it's going to interfere with your sense of duty – of loyalty.'

Oppenheimer closed his eyes. Groves's tone became gentle, almost paternal. Now was the time to apply pressure – without giving Oppenheimer room to manoeuvre. 'You're going to have to decide. Put it on the scales. Think logically – without sentiment.'

When Oppie opened his eyes again he peered out across the Washington lawns. There she stood, in that bright, floral dress she wore to the beach. There she stood, letting the wind sweep her hair back, wrapping her dress round her slight frame. Staring straight into the car. Straight into his soul. Jean. He dropped his head into his hands and for a moment felt he was going mad. Her name rolled around his mouth, he wanted to scream it aloud. But when he looked up, there were only the trees, the grass and a woman with her dog.

His shoulders sagged. 'No one's going to allow this to be aborted, are they?'

Groves decided it was time to give Oppenheimer a dose of the real world: cold and hard. 'No, we are not. Are you with us, or against us?'

Oppenheimer wouldn't answer. The general switched gears, setting a more personal scene now. 'I'm like a turtle. I'll stick my head out because that's the only way to get anywhere. But I'm certainly not going to sit in front of some senate inquiry in a couple of years' time, trying to explain why I spent $1.9 billion of other people's money on a show that didn't open.' Oppenheimer looked across at the general, who stared back at him. His voice became urgent. 'You've got just one thing to do. Just give me that bomb. Give it to me, Doctor, and I'll take care of the rest.'

That evening they presented a united front when they both turned up at the Folger Theatre. It was a typical Washington function, plenty of brass rubbing shoulders with diplomats and politicians. They were guests of 'Colonel' Stimson and his wife, with seats in the front row of the circle for a performance of *The Sorcerer's Apprentice*. No one imagined Groves would have had much of an eye for ballet, but he revelled in it. What he saw, presented before him, was the results of immaculate team-work: orchestra, lights and talent. This was the sort of thing he loved – hard work, precision, dedication, all going to create a tangible result, something greater than the sum of its parts. Strangely, he felt at home here. When an usher leaned over and tapped him on the shoulder, he had the look of a man who'd been awakened from the perfect dream.

He read the note that had been slipped to him and he frowned. Then after making his apologies to the 'Colonel' and his wife, he made his way out. Oppenheimer looked up quizzically, but the general dismissed the mute inquiry with a shake of his head.

Doug Panton paced up and down the deserted foyer. He was an intelligence officer acting as liaison between Groves's command and the Joint Intelligence Chiefs. It was the JIC's job to chew over the latest reports and feed them in a digestible form to the president, the Combined Chiefs of Staff and the commanders in the field. Panton was Groves's guarantee that he would not be the last one in line.

'What is it, Doug?'

'I'm sorry to disturb you, sir. I thought we ought to bring you up to date and this is the only chance I had. You know the Japanese have been putting out peace feelers?'

'I'd heard something.'

'Well, we've been intercepting their messages to Moscow. They've been trying to use the Russians as go-betweens. So far the Russians haven't been too interested.'

Groves, expressionless, watched a group of Soviet generals strolling across the empty foyer. 'Hardly surprising . . .'

'The thing is, General, recently, US secret agents have intercepted Japanese contacts with representatives of Switzerland and Portugal. They want to negotiate terms for surrender.'

'What kind of terms? Unconditional surrender?'

'The main condition seems to be reassurances about the future of the emperor . . .'

'Is it unconditional?'

'Well, no, sir – I just explained.'

'Well, then, no one's going to buy it.'

Panton wiped his forehead with a handkerchief and returned it to his pocket. 'I just thought you ought to be put in the picture, General,' he repeated stubbornly. 'There is a lot of lobbying going on down here, to let the Japanese off the hook about the emperor.'

'*What?*'

'Acting Secretary of State Grew – he used to be Ambassador to Tokyo – is holding meetings with all the cabinet. He's seen the president twice now. He keeps going on about letting the Japs know there's no problem about the emperor – says it's the only way they'll stop fighting.'

'Grew's an appeaser. It makes my blood boil to hear this.'

'I should tell you, sir, he's won more than a few hearts and minds.'

'Look, if it isn't unconditional surrender, we've got nothing to worry about.'

Groves slipped back to his seat and sat quietly through the rest of the show, although it could have been a three-ring circus for all he saw of it now. He turned the elements of what he'd just been told over and over in his mind. Would the politicians really steal his thunder? Was there a chance they might negotiate? Was it really possible after all the time and money he'd seen spent? He glanced along the line of faces: Oppenheimer's, the 'Colonel's' and the Soviet delegation at the end of the row.

Outside, rain had swept the streets, leaving everything as if decorated in a thousand jewels. As they gathered on the steps of the theatre, waiting for the limousines, Groves managed to share an umbrella with the old 'Colonel'.

'Mr Secretary, may I ask a blunt question?' Stimson looked up at Groves. 'Are you and the president still considering accepting Russian help in the war against Japan?'

'It's not a question of accepting anything. Back in 1944 we asked the Russians to come in. At Yalta last February Stalin gave us a guarantee – three months after Germany surrendered, they would attack Japan.'

'That makes it 8 August.'

'Yes, 8 August,' echoed Stimson, 'That's the date to keep your eye on.'

Groves breathed in the damp air and sensed Stimson and he might be on the same wave-length. 'With respect, Mr Secretary, do we really need Russian help to defeat Japan?'

'Back in 1944, we thought we would. Now? Well, you've read the same reports I have, General. Japan's finished and she knows it.'

'But if we don't need Russian help?'

'Oh, they'll come in anyway – for their own reasons. It won't matter to them whether we want them in or not. They have a very old score to settle with the Japanese, one that goes back to 1907. You probably don't remember that.'

Stimson took hold of the general's arm and squeezed

it – half out of good humour and half to steady himself. Groves looked down at the old man, at the exhausted eyes, the cheeks that had collapsed, the mouth perpetually wet with saliva. It was hard to believe Henry Stimson had also been Secretary for War during the First World War. Now here he was, one of the greatest pillars of the eastern establishment, clinging on to the general just like any old man with unsteady legs.

'Mr Secretary, I'd wager the Russians also have their eye on Manchuria.'

'My dear General, the Russians have their eye on Manchuria, Mongolia, China and Korea. They want warm-water ports in the Pacific – and they also expect to share in the actual occupation of Japan.'

Stimson looked up at the general again. This time he seemed even older than his seventy-six years. But Groves felt they both understood each other, so he said what he assumed the 'Colonel' wanted to hear. 'I'm sure you appreciate, Mr Secretary, that the gadget would probably keep the Russians out of Japan. And give the president a big stick to wave at Stalin ...'

'You're talking about our Allies, General.' The rebuke stung Groves, but he took it on the chin.

'For now, Mr Secretary ...'

Stimson stepped down into the street and peered towards the lights for a sign of his car. He also glanced across at the women huddled together under the street lamp. The old man was checking for eavesdroppers. 'General. Let me remind you of two dates: the first one is 8 August. If we're going to limit Soviet ambitions, that's the date you have to aim for.' Groves nodded. The old man had been way ahead of him.

'The second date is far more critical – and far more imperative. The president goes to Potsdam to meet with Stalin in mid-July. He's already postponed the meeting by two weeks to give you more time. He can't afford another postponement. Now, the president would like to know whether the "gadget" actually works before he sits down with Joseph Stalin.'

'No problem, Mr Secretary, we'll be right –'

'I've had reports that some of your scientists are less than completely committed. I hear they have some moral qualms about their work. You know Dr Szilard has tried to see the president, and I understand there's some kind of petition . . .'

Suddenly the general understood that although an old man might sometimes lean on a younger man's arm, he doesn't mean anything by it. 'I hadn't heard about that, sir, I'll look into it. They're all under stress.' He wanted some understanding, but he wasn't about to get it.

A heavy black Cadillac cruised up to the curb, the Secretary and his wife stepped inside and said good-night. Groves needed to punish someone. Bronson cruised the Buick up to the same curb a moment later and Mrs Groves was shepherded out of the way. Groves looked around him. 'Doug!'

Panton hurried over from the steps of the theatre.

'When you interrogated Dr Oppenheimer over those attempted contacts, you know, the espionage attempts,' Panton knew, 'we got one name from him, right?'

'That's right.'

'But there were three contacts. Did you ever get the other names out of him?'

'No sir.'

'Well, press for them. He needs to feel his branch creak a little.'

FOURTEEN

The week that Oppenheimer was in Washington with Groves, Richard Shoenfield had decided to take a vacation to visit his folks. At least, that's what he told the WAC who had issued him with his pass. In fact, he rented a car and drove cross-country. East, to Tennessee. From Knoxville, he took the road that follows the Clinch River to the new township they called Oak Ridge. He'd seen the name on the buff-coloured file in Groves's safe, the night he and Merriman had planted the banana skin. As he came round the last bend in the road he took his foot off the gas and just let it coast to a stop under an old paper-bark tree.

'Holy shit!'

There it was. In three years it had grown from nothing, and now it rose like a great city of the plain. Stretching towards the horizon was a site that made Los Alamos seem like a little country village. Four massive rectangular complexes, grouped together inside acres and acres of barbed-wire fences. This was where they extracted purified uranium – on a site that had the unmistakable look of absolute permanence.

Oppenheimer raised a glass of thin, white California

Chardonnay and watched the light play against the golden liquid.

'The Chicago group have suggested,' he took a polite sip, 'that we demonstrate the gadget to the Japanese.'

Groves put down his glass of iced water. 'Lord protect us from our enemies without and our Hungarians within.' He had taken Oppenheimer to his favourite restaurant, a popular watering hole of the military on the Pentagon side of the river. It was a great barn of a place, filled to capacity with wall-to-wall khaki and resounding to the trumpetings of warriors home from the hill.

'It's an idea that has its attractions. We lay on a demonstration on some uninhabited Japanese atoll ...'

'Doctor, you're from a privileged background, aren't you?'

'What?'

'Optimism. Your faith in the positive qualities of humanity. I didn't have much of that when I was a kid. I remember the realities. We didn't get a wake-up call at Pearl Harbor.'

'Are you saying we should extinguish a Japanese city as revenge for Pearl Harbor?'

Groves chewed both his food and the thought over carefully. 'No. Like I said, I'm a realist. What if it's a dud? What if the Japanese ship a load of Allied POWs into the drop zone?'

Now it was Oppenheimer's turn to think it over. 'The idea should go to the president, at least.'

'Where do you come off mouthing these ideas?' Groves decided that a tough-guy stance was the only way to make it clear to Oppie where he stood. 'Those guys in security have a right to ask where these ideas come from. Demonstration!' He spat the word out like a piece of gristle. 'Stopping production, sharing our work with the Soviets!' He took another mouthful of water. 'See it from their point of view. How are you going to convince them that this stuff is only coming out of Chicago? I'll tell you what it sounds like, it sounds foreign, subversive.'

Oppenheimer realized that he was listening to the voice of middle America. He never ceased to be amazed by the parochial twang of its sentiments, but he was aware that he was in the minority and that Groves's ideas were the kind that shaped American policy. 'I thought the idea simply sounded moral.'

'Moral? Was the slaughter of British hospital staff in Singapore moral? Was Buchenwald moral? Demonstration? I say we show the enemy in the harshest possible way that we play in the same league as they do.

'When we sit down in that committee room, we're going to debate the whole idea of a "demonstration". Then the committee is going to send a recommendation to the president. Now, you can help yourself here.' Groves took up the same tack that had proved so successful before when Oppenheimer was being recalcitrant. 'It's going to come down to one thing – are you for us, or against us?'

Oppenheimer havered. 'My mind's not made up yet.'

'Well, think about this. Are you going to help yourself and your colleagues out in New Mexico, or are you going to stick yourself right out on the end of a limb?' He repeated his main point, jabbing with his fork for emphasis: 'You're either for us, or against us. I don't see it any other way.' Groves stared deep into Oppenheimer's head, as though he were drilling the words home. Then there was the briefest flick of the eye and his face radiated with pleasure. 'Brehon!' Bearing down on their table was General Brehon Sommervell. Groves sprang to his feet. 'General Sommervell, I want you to meet Dr Robert Oppenheimer. This here's a great man.' The general pumped Oppenheimer's arm and beamed at the two of them.

'Dr Oppenheimer. I've heard terrific things about you. God damn it, Dick, I hear we're all going to be grateful to your Dr Oppenheimer pretty soon. They tell me, Doctor, you've got something to shake those Japs right out of their trees. A lot of people are going to be glad to get out of this war. Doctor, I'm proud to shake your hand.'

Sommervell left as quickly as he'd arrived and Groves took up his fork, still shooting looks of approval at Oppenheimer. 'Think about what he just said. You see it right tomorrow and this country will owe you – soldier.'

Shoenfield got the full treatment. A visiting medic from Los Alamos, someone from the very nerve centre of the whole great adventure – they were delighted to see him. He was shepherded by a young doctor past some aerial photographs of the site: one taken in 1941 of soft rolling fields beside the Clinch River, and one taken in 1944.

'Doesn't seem possible, does it?'

Shoenfield could only nod.

'God knows why they called it Oak Ridge. There's no ridge that I've ever seen and the nearest oaks must be way up in Michigan.'

'Just how big –'

'Pretty big – 85,000 employees, all in here.' He waved his hand at the photograph. 'The whole thing to date has cost upwards of $500 million.'

'Good God!' Shoenfield shook his head. They were coasting down the cleanest, shiniest corridor that he had ever seen. 'What's in here?'

'Just a ward.'

'Project R?' The young doctor brought himself to a halt and turned on Shoenfield. Richard was ready for him. 'It's OK, we see your data at Los Alamos. I'm doing the same work with animals.'

'Oh, right.' The doctor beamed with genuine delight. 'See, the whole thing's so compartmentalized – we didn't know you guys were doing the same experiments.'

'You're so right. No one knows what anyone else is doing. Crazy, huh?'

The young doctor leaned against a pair of swing-doors and led him into an isolation ward. Shoenfield took a deep breath but kept his emotions under control. At the end of the room were two figures. He moved closer to get a better look. One, an old man, sat drooling, his arm quivering uncontrollably. The other was a malnourished young girl.

'What have you been dosing them with?'

'The old guy, 60,000 Pico curies. The girl, I'm not sure.' He crossed to the clip-file hanging above her bed. The two of them seemed utterly insensible. 'Right, here we are. She's had 6 million Pico curies.

Of plutonium, that is. That's ninety-eight times the maximum acceptable level.'

'Only ninety-eight times . . .' Shoenfield's tone suggested that he had just been told an interesting – but unsurprising – detail. In fact, he could barely keep from screaming.

The doctor was pleased to have such an interested audience, and went on: 'We had five patients here before. We get no follow-ups. Not that I can find.'

'And no consent forms, either.'

The young man slapped the clip-file back on to its hook and answered without thinking: 'Well, how were they going to sign them, with an X?'

Shoenfield's eyes had widened, which made the doctor turn. There was movement behind him. The girl had doubled over, but there was nothing either of them could do to stop her vomiting a great wave of green bile all across the floor.

The committee sat for two days in a cedar-panelled room next to the 'Colonel's' office in the Pentagon. On the first day they discussed the possibility of inviting a couple of prominent Soviet scientists to witness the test, a proposal which had been tabled earlier. A committee member said he respected the Soviets, he thought they were not as bad as people claimed. Groves almost choked, especially when Fermi and Oppenheimer all agreed the idea would show good faith. But he soon relaxed again: there were some politicians at the table, and they showed the good sense to bury the idea.

Then Stimson steered the conversation towards whether the Japanese should be warned about the 'gadget' before its proposed use. It was the Under-Secretary for the Navy who spoke most strongly for a warning. Tuckson was a quiet man of high principle, one of those career servicemen who had been taught from a military manual most people thought was out of print.

'Our intelligence is saying that when the Russians declare war on Japan it'll knock them out of the war. I believe the Japanese are susceptible to reason, much more than our press wants to admit. They are not a nation of mad fanatics. Their history shows the opposite. I feel certain these extraordinary acts of suicide are largely based on their belief that we mean to execute their emperor. They genuinely think they are fighting to save his life.' The room hummed with unspoken tension, and Tuckson felt himself to be alone. 'This weapon will kill tens of thousands of civilians. I was not taught to wage war in that manner.'

Groves leaned towards Stimson and murmured, 'If Custer had used the machine-gun, his history would have been written differently.' The 'Colonel' wasn't sure he had heard the man properly and simply stared at him blankly. But Groves wasn't going to repeat himself, and Tuckson wasn't finished.

'If we go ahead, particularly if we use this weapon without any prior warning, I shall not only resign from this committee, but from my office in the Department – and my commission.' Tuckson checked his watch. 'Now, if you will excuse me, gentlemen . . .'

After a decent pause, Stimson suggested they take a break for some coffee. Groves watched Oppenheimer intently, while giving the impression that his mind was elsewhere. As they stood by the buffet table, stirring their coffee, the 'Colonel', almost absent-mindedly, raised the issue of demonstration.

'Dr Oppenheimer?' In the silence that followed only the tinkle of sterling silver against bone china could be heard. Oppenheimer returned to the safety of the table, clutching a small sandwich in his hand, before he answered. Groves's eyes never left his face.

'Well, logically, the dropping of this weapon is implicit in the entire project.' He avoided looking across at the general. He wanted no coaching, no approval, no recriminations. 'Let's suppose we mount a demonstration.' Groves was trying to appear confident. 'There's always the possibility that it might fail. Then the whole exercise would have been a waste of time.' Oppenheimer took a bite from his sandwich. Still he kept his eyes on his coffee cup, but Groves was looking approvingly at his bent head. 'We need to keep in mind that we're not going to have an assembly line producing these things. Our projected capacity is one device by mid-July for the test, another one by 1 August and perhaps a third a little later. Now, if we use one up on the demonstration and it fails, we're desperately short of gadgets.' Fermi looked on like a choir boy at confession. 'Besides, can anyone be certain a demonstration would induce the Japanese to surrender?'

Groves settled deeper into his seat. His boy had passed his first test. The politicians waded in and gave the discussion a little more focus, but from that moment the whole process ran smoothly to the end.

Stimson summed it all up: 'So, the recommendation I will give the president is that the S–1 be used as soon as possible and that it be used without warning. To avoid the unnecesssary killing of civilians, the target will be a major military establishment, employing a great many workers, closely surrounded by workers' houses. It is our purpose to inflict a profound psychological impact on as many of the inhabitants as possible.'

Oppenheimer closed his eyes and ran the contradictions through his head. How could they avoid the unnecessary killing of civilians, while at the same time trying to inflict a profound psychological impact on as many people as possible? They were aiming for a target 'closely surrounded by workers' houses'. It was either madness, or it was a lie. When he opened his eyes again, Stimson was in the process of taking a vote. All around him, there were hands raised to say 'aye'. Stimson counted them round the table and then arrived at Oppenheimer – whose hand was in the air. Oppenheimer looked across at Groves, who gave him the smallest of nods.

FIFTEEN

Szilard took Merriman on a tour of the lab and then brought him back to his room at the Quadrangle Faculty Club at the University of Chicago. Szilard had been there for the past three years, living out of the same two suitcases. At the club he handed Merriman an envelope.

'It's not sealed. You can read it if you like.'

'Maybe on the train.'

'Atrocious things have been done in Germany in this war because people there didn't speak out – and now we blame them for it. Correctly, I think, even though it might have been dangerous. Well, it's not dangerous for us to speak out. A lot of us here feel that we have a great responsibility.' He sensed that Merriman was a less than willing courier and stopped his lecture. He smiled and shrugged. 'You don't have to agree with its contents, Michael. You just have to agree it should be discussed.'

Merriman looked at him intently, then slid the envelope into his briefcase.

Merriman boarded the train back to Santa Fe and settled himself into his compartment. On the rack above his head he had placed the lead-lined case carrying core fragments from the lab, his suitcase and, beside it, the briefcase with Szilard's petition. He threw his feet up on the seat opposite and wondered about what he was carrying. He took out the envelope and read the first page.

> WE ARE IN A COMPLETELY DIFFERENT SITUATION THAT CANNOT BE RESOLVED BY WAR.

He was tired, his eyes were aching, but he turned the page.

Down in the reserved section of the train, a party was just getting under way. Pash, long back from Germany, and now assigned to the staff at Los Alamos, was occupied with his role as bartender. De Silva and Latrobe had already greased the wheels.

'Isn't anyone going to give me a seltzer?' complained the general.

'It's a tough assignment, but someone's got to do it.' Pash handed him a glass and the two men dissolved into peals of laughter.

Then the general began musing aloud. 'You know what's got ahold of me?' Pash shook his head. 'Six hundred thousand men, three plants as big as cities. There is nothing and nobody that can stop us now. Not you, not even me.

'You know, de Silva, you only scratched the surface with all your reports. You never understood the boy wonder. He wants to dazzle, that's what he wants – to be king of the mountain. He'd never betray this country. You know why? Because that would take him out of the limelight. And that's the one thing he will never stand for. He'd kill anyone who blocked his way to the top – and that's where he'll end up: the top. Never mind, gentlemen. He'll deserve it.' Groves raised his seltzer. 'Here's to us. Just don't expect any gratitude.'

Once the committee's deliberations were out of the way, the project moved ahead with ominous speed. There was a sudden frisson round the site the day they rolled open the great doors of the ordnance shop. No one could quite believe how far down the line they had travelled. For years they had seemed to be in a hopeless race to keep up with a punishing schedule. Now the race seemed to be rolling away from them under its own steam.

That was the day they decided to transport the basic un-armed gadget out to the final assembly based at Trinity. As the doors of the shop clanged open, the inner workings of the great secret were suddenly flooded by cruel daylight. Inside, where the empty 'Fat Man' and 'Little Boy' casings had once hung, a large, clumsy-looking steel ball was hoisted into the air and laid upon a waiting truck. Jeep drivers and motorcyclists stood about as sentries. As the vehicle crept into the sunlight bearing its load like the rock of ages, the escorts slipped into their pre-arranged ranks and proceeded at a snail's pace down the road.

Sitting in a jeep with Kathleen, Merriman watched this procession roll by. Since his return from Chicago he had seemed somehow lost, distracted and confused.

'It's coming close, whatever it is you're working on, isn't it?'

Merriman took a sip of some coffee they were sharing from a flask and nodded.

'I can feel it pressing down on everybody,' Kathleen said. 'Something's going to happen soon. It's got everybody worked up.'

Merriman had no words to add.

'There's been a run on sleeping pills, aspirin. Look, I know you can't talk about it.'

'I can't.'

'There's something else though, isn't there?' Merriman looked across at her as though she'd just twisted his heart. 'Talk to Dr Oppenheimer. If anyone has thought it through, it'll be him.' She let her words drift away, taking his hand and caressing it. Then, 'Touch me.'

Merriman gently ran his finger down her cheek – and down to her neck. He slipped his arm round her waist and pulled her to him. Her arms encircled his shoulders and she moved her mouth close to his ear.

'Naked. Isn't that a beautiful word?'

He buried his face in her hair and breathed in her scent.

'Tonight.' She put her mouth to his cheek and tasted his flesh. 'I want to make love.'

'Kathleen . . .'

She released herself from his arms and got to her feet. 'And I want a future. That's what I really want. You and me.'

Merriman caught up with Oppenheimer in the explosives workshop at the Omega Site. He and Kistiakowsky were standing over a pallet of explosive wedges. 'For God's sake, it's pitted again. They've failed almost every time so far, Kisty. They fail on the test and it'll be your department that lets the whole project down,' said Oppenheimer, close to hysteria.

Merriman kept his distance. He had walked right into the middle of a crisis. Oppenheimer was supervising the preparation of the explosive wedges for the 'Fat Man' weapon. In order to produce exactly the right shape for each wedge, they were being made from a series of precision moulds. But this process raised the problem of escaping air from the molten explosive material, which left the surface pitted and uneven. The very slightest deviation from the required shape meant the difference between success and disaster.

Kisty understood the problem even more clearly than Oppenheimer. 'We'll have to use hand-lathing. I can't think of any other way.'

Oppenheimer had stretched himself and was rubbing his eyes. He caught sight of Merriman standing by the door and was annoyed that this problem, and his reaction to it, had been witnessed. 'Want something?'

Merriman crossed to where Oppenheimer was standing, holding the envelope before him. 'From Chicago, you know – Szilard.' Oppenheimer was still looking down at the wedges and tossed a shrug at Kisty. He took the envelope almost absent-mindedly as Merriman continued: 'I read it on the train.'

Oppie suddenly saw himself, fifteen years younger. He said gently, 'And what do you think?'

'It unnerved me. Are we going to discuss it? I mean, are you going to discuss it with us?' Oppenheimer looked down at the floor and waited for the stumbling speech to cease. 'Are we going on?'

Oppenheimer said softly, 'I don't see anyone stopping it.' Merriman looked across at the stack of explosives, but he wanted a clearer answer. 'Look, Michael, all we've been asked to do is solve a technical problem. It doesn't give us a voice on how it should be used.' From behind his head the phone jangled and Kisty grabbed it from the wall. 'I have thought about this . . .'

'Oppie, it's for you. Goethe's got revised figures!'

'Be right there. Listen, Michael, leave it with me.' He started for the phone, then turned back on his heel. 'The initiator will be delivered in a few hours. We'll need your test results pronto.'

Groves had taken the opportunity to get away from the minutiae of the whole operation. He was tired of problems with initiators and ignition coils. He wanted to get ahold of the big picture. So he took a trip down to Knoxville Air Base in Tennessee, to take a flight in the latest B29, the aircraft chosen to carry the first nuclear weapon into battle.

They'd taken the machine up to cruising height and then allowed Groves to slip into the co-pilot's chair. The B29, though a remarkable piece of work, was prone to engine fires. Groves wanted to hear all the complaints up front, before it was too late.

'See, the top cylinder overheats and that gives us valve failure,' the pilot explained.

'So how would you fix it?'

'I'd ask for fuel injection to replace carburettors. I'd also want the airframe lightened; no sense in carrying any unnecessary weight.'

'Right.'

'I'd also want reversible electric propellers, and generally to beef up the power, even if we don't need it . . .'

'Just make up your list and send it through. I'll see that it gets done. I'm going in back to talk to the bombardier.'

He moved through the pressurized cockpit, into the tube that ran towards the middle and rear gunners. He climbed out into the bomb-bay area where he found the man he was looking for standing on a narrow footway that ran on either side of the frame. He held some blueprints in his hands and was trying to envisage 'Fat Man' in position.

'Hi there!' Groves yelled above the engine noise.

The bombardier saluted. 'We're gonna need to redesign this section, cut away some of the pressurized tunnel. Put in quick closing pneumatic bomb-bay doors. It's a tall order, General.'

'Great, I love 'em! I'll get it done, don't worry. Open the doors, will you?' The bombardier took hold of the manual lever and pulled it towards him. The wind struck suddenly and the entire world seemed to be at his feet. The general let out an hysterical howl, but it was lost in the wind.

'How high are we?' he screamed into the young man's ear.

'Just about 8,000 feet. We're at 80 per cent power.'

Groves stared out across Tennessee and felt like God. 'Man is an awesome creature,' he said.

At the Omega site Merriman got down to the job he was paid for, tickling the dragon's tail. He was still trying to perfect the correct weight and mass for plutonium, but he was trying it a new way. He now had two half spheres of a plutonium core separated by two screwdrivers. As he lifted or lowered the frail tools, bringing the spheres further away from – or closer to – critical mass, the monitoring equipment gave him his readings, the Geiger counters testifying to the background radiation. The tense expressions on everyone's faces confirmed the ever-present danger.

Merriman waited a moment, remembering something Wilson had said about how, towards the climax of a project, everything seems to speed up, rush to the conclusion. Wait, he'd said. Check everything again. Merriman did. It was all fine.

He manipulated the assembly. Then, over his shoulder to a young man in shirt-sleeves: 'Take notes, will you?' He knew he was close to the all-important answer. The monitors screamed a warning. 'Are you taking the readings, for God's sake?' Merriman's voice cracked with anxiety.

'Here's the log, here it is.' The young scientist snatched at it in relief. He grabbed futilely as he saw the coffee cup that had been sitting on one corner of the log tilt over and, almost in slow motion, fall to the floor and shatter.

The crash, because unexpected, seemed hideously loud. Merriman jumped and the two half spheres of plutonium fell together. The monitors roared up to a high-pitched whine as the core temperatures soared. The air was 'cooked' and the room was filled with an eerie blue light – all in less than a second. Merriman knew that he was staring into the face of the dragon.

A voice screamed, 'Critical, critical!'

Merriman instinctively punched the deadly assembly apart with his bare hands. The temperature dropped and the light faded.

When everything had stopped, when the monitors stopped their terrible noise, when the measuring equipment had shut down, the scientist stood rooted to the spot, stunned. Merriman's hand felt as though it had been pierced by a thousand needles. His tongue felt prickly – the first symptom of a massive dose of radiation.

He shouted, 'Nobody move! Don't anybody move!'

He stepped to the blackboard and took a piece of chalk, broke it into pieces and handed each person a piece. 'Everyone mark the place where they were standing – then get out.'

By the time the army ambulances and the head of security had arrived, Merriman had almost finished his calculations. On the floor were the ghostly outlines of five pairs of feet, and from each a line was drawn towards the dragon. On the blackboard Merriman had written the name of each scientist, and underneath he had calculated the radiation dose that they had each received. Standing just behind his shoulder was the young man in shirt-sleeves. He had been standing nearest to Merriman at the time.

His calculations complete, Merriman stared at the blackboard. Then he turned to his companion and smiled.

'Looks like you should all make it.' He tossed the chalk aside. 'Except for me . . . I'm dead.'

SIXTEEN

When Shoenfield finally got back to Los Alamos, he ran straight to the dorm looking for Merriman. His head was filled with his news from Oak Ridge and he was bursting to talk to someone. He jogged up to the lodge, but no one had seen Merriman there. Wilson thought he'd probably still be up at Omega. So Shoenfield took off in that direction. As he got closer to the site he was overtaken by jeeps and cars chasing up the hill, then an ambulance tearing away in the opposite direction, followed by another jeep, which suddenly braked and skidded in the gravel. Out of it jumped an MP.

'Dr Shoenfield! We've been looking for you all over!' Shoenfield ran up. 'We've had an accident.'

'What kind of accident?'

'A bad allergy.'

'Who?'

'Merriman.'

'Michael?' Shoenfield leaped into the jeep. 'Let's go, let's go!'

Kathleen had been on duty and had just taken a moment to go downstairs to fetch the drugs' trolley. Suddenly from behind her the doors to the ward were flung open and Merriman, his shirt-sleeved companion and a gang of doctors charged down the corridor.

'What's the matter, darling?'

'Nothing, no problem.' He didn't even look at her. Just swept past with his entourage.

Behind them flowed a second wave: Shoenfield and the security chief, together with a couple of MPs. Now she knew it was serious. 'Richard . . .?'

Shoenfield waved her aside and grasped hold of one of the doctors trailing behind Merriman. 'How much?'

'About 1,000 rads, he says.' Richard whitened.

Kathleen had caught up with them. 'Richard, what's happening? What is it, for God's sake?' Richard came to a halt, but couldn't manage to look at her.

'Michael, we're going to see what we can do. Everything's under control. I'll do everything I can.'

Kathleen felt terror take her by the throat.

The security chief brushed past them, took hold of a lieutenant and led him to one side. He hissed into his ear: 'I want this whole wing closed down, and I think we should think about getting some military doctors.'

No one out at Trinity that day knew anything about the Omega Site incident. They were all concentrating on the imminent arrival of a very precious cargo. As Merriman was in the throes of his dance with death, 200 miles away they were waiting to assemble the greatest instrument of destruction man had ever created. Groves had placed guards all round the perimeter, in the event of an attack from Japanese commandos.

Five thousand yards from the Trinity tower, along the road leading up to the Macdonald Ranch House, came a convoy of vehicles, escorted by motorcycle outriders. In the midst of the convoy was an ambulance that cruised up to the front porch and stopped. The back doors were opened and from inside two scientists emerged carrying a steel canister.

Inside the ranch house the assembly team were dressed in surgeons' gowns and masks. To one side stood the military, represented by General Farrel and his aides. Representing the Eggheads was Norbert Harper. He approached the general with some papers and a pen.

'Some things for you to sign, General.'

'What are they?'

'They say that the University of California is hereby handing over the plutonium core of a nuclear device to the United States Army. Or to put it simply, it's a bill for $2 billion.' Before Farrel would sign he asked to see inside the canister. Harper was delighted. He handed the general a pair of rubber gloves. Then, as he eased open the lid, the nearest Geiger counter let out a shiver.

Oppenheimer had been out by the tower, supervising the details of the electrical control systems. He emerged from a local dust-storm that had stirred up the powdery surface beneath the tower to answer a call from General Groves. Oppenheimer wrenched a pair of small goggles from his head and paused by the mobile communications vehicle. In the back, a young RT operator was holding a handset out to the doctor.

'He's patched in from Tennessee.'

Oppenheimer climbed up on to the truck and took the handset. 'Dr Oppenheimer. Yes, General. Uh-huh. Uh-huh. Yeah, there's another hold-up.' He changed the receiver to his other hand. 'Well, basically it's detonation circuits, now. I don't know. I need another 24 hours. One more day.'

He listened to the general at the other end and his expression became confused. 'I don't see the connection. Merriman brought a copy the other day from Chicago. Some physicists have signed it.'

While Oppenheimer stood in the middle of a dust-storm, Groves was getting drenched in a shower. He had commandeered a radio-telephone facility in the middle of Knoxville Field that offered virtually no shelter. He yelled above the noise of the rain on a tin roof and taxiing aircraft. 'Those pinkos – won't they ever go away? I swear, if we ever get the thing to work, I'm gonna drop it on Chicago. I'll intern those longhairs! If I hear about this again, I swear I will! I hear you, do you hear me? Finish it, that's an order! Listen, I have a plane to catch. I'll be there in 48 hours.'

He pulled his raincoat tighter, seemingly trying to cut himself in two as he tightened the belt. He turned to Latrobe, who was jerking his thumb towards an aircraft standing by. For the first time he seemed genuinely angry, rather than using his anger to produce a result. 'Every time I turn around, somebody gets to him. I'm certain they're trying for a postponement. I will *not* allow it.'

'Could also be a million other things. The weather, technical.'

'Out of the question.' He snatched his briefcase and

opened it. From it he took a telex which he thrust at Latrobe. Marked SECRET, and dated 13 July it read:

> TRUMAN, BYRNES AND STIMSON ARRIVE POTSDAM TOMORROW FOR CONFERENCE WITH STALIN. ADVISE RESULTS OF TRINITY TEST SOONEST.

'The old man knows how to turn up the pressure,' Latrobe commented.

'There's only one country that can hold back the flood-waters of Communism, and God has given us the chance to avail ourselves of the most powerful weapon known to man.' Latrobe watched the general stand staring into space in the pouring rain. He felt utterly impotent, until suddenly Groves turned to him, confident again: 'And God has blessed us with the guts to use it. Before Truman sits down with Uncle Joe this thing has got to go up. Because Stalin could cut Truman down with two fingers. The president's got to walk in there carrying a baseball bat!'

And Groves clambered up the steps to the waiting aircraft.

At the Los Alamos Hospital a life was trickling away. Shoenfield and his colleagues were going over the latest batch of X-rays, which resembled specimens from some macabre experiment. None of them had ever seen anything like it before.

'The heart looks larger. Do you think there's fluid in the pericardial sac?' Shoenfield asked.

'Who knows? Radiation induced?'

'Probably. Where are yesterday's pictures?' They really were in the dark.

'Is he lucid?'

'In and out. The brain has swelled tremendously from the radiation.'

'What happens next?'

They all looked at Shoenfield.

'I don't know. I really have no idea. No human being has ever received this dose of radiation before. He is dying, that's for sure – but from the inside out.'

Shoenfield left them to it. He stood at the door as one of his colleagues laid out some further data: 'There are other problems to contend with. The GI tracts have been destroyed by radiation.'

Shoenfield pushed against the door and stumbled straight into Kathleen. She looked at him, desperately needing some news. 'We are doing everything we can.' He put his arm around her shoulders and steered her back down the corridor. 'Absolutely everything. Now, it's not going to help him to have you fall apart. Give yourself a break and go home.'

She pulled herself free. 'I can't, Richard. Don't ask me, I just can't.'

Gradually a sense of disorientation had crept over Kathleen. The corridor, emergency, the examination areas that had been her domain for the last three years had gradually become unfamiliar, strange, alien. She walked towards the large exit sign, uncertain where she was or where she was going. For the first time since she was a child, Kathleen was lost.

Behind her a pair of swing-doors burst apart and a brace of medics emerged, wheeling a patient on a theatre-trolley. A stranger, an unknown figure – but it couldn't be. Michael? In the second as they passed her she caught a glimpse of the man whose flesh she had tasted just hours ago. She followed the trolley, staring at the creature upon it. Beneath a swinging bottle of plasma, Michael's arms were packed in ice: his hands had inflated like rubber gloves. On one side of his face a dark beard had appeared, on the other, his hair had completely gone. She looked at the face and the skin seemed to be boiling off the bone. She could barely control the scream that had begun to swell inside her. He could not see her. His eyes had haemorrhaged. He was blind.

In the driving rain Oppenheimer's car swept up to the entrance to the hospital. He leaped out of the back and charged towards the doors, but was halted by an MP, heavily armed. A security officer stepped out to join them in the pouring rain.

'Why wasn't I told?' demanded Oppenheimer.

'Too much panic,' the man said laconically.

'How is he?'

'I'm not the one to ask.'

'I'd like to see him.'

'We're not permitting visitors,' explained the security officer, but Oppenheimer hadn't heard him. 'The men who were with him have been spoken to. They understand. This is a delicate time, Doctor.' Oppenheimer re-focused on the man in uniform. 'Goddam it, I'm the project director!' He got no response.

At that moment Shoenfield came out, and Oppenheimer leaped at him: 'Richard. How is he? Is he conscious?'

'He's in and out. He wants to know . . .' He paused, almost uncertain how to put it.

Oppenheimer stood helpless. 'Yes?'

'Have you read the Chicago petition? It means a lot to him.'

Oppenheimer's answer, a mumbled 'yes', was almost swept away with the rain.

'That's it? Is that all?' Shoenfield strengthened his resolve. 'Yes I have, and I wash my hands of it? Now wait a minute, Oppenheimer. I've got a friend falling apart in there. He thinks you've got all the answers, because that's what you let him think.' Oppenheimer steadied himself against the torrent. This was the last thing he had expected. Shoenfield stepped closer. 'Now, do you really know what the hell is going on here or is the whole thing totally out of control?'

'Are you trying to make a particular point?'

'Yes, yes I am.' Shoenfield's anger was spilling out of him now. 'I've spent the past two years of my life putting up with all your security, secrecy and control – and now I don't think that all that bullshit is meant to keep what's going on here from the enemy. I think it's to keep it from ordinary Americans. They just might not like what's going on here.'

Oppenheimer looked down at his boots. Then he snapped back at Shoenfield: 'Ordinary American people don't want to know what we're doing here. All they really care is that their sons come home alive. And I'm doing everything in my power to see that they do.'

Shoenfield stepped out into the rain and pointed out towards the east. 'Like at Oak Ridge, where they're injecting uncomprehending people with huge doses of plutonium?'

Oppenheimer didn't want to hear this now. 'I don't know anything about Oak Ridge.' Then he recovered himself. 'But if you want to ask me a question about what's going on here, ask this: will it be big enough? Is it going to be big enough to scare the wits out of all of us? To make us stop and think, my God, is this what we can do? Will it be big enough to make us stop all war forever? If you want to ask a question, ask that.'

'Is that what you ask yourself? Well, let me tell you something. I've seen Oak Ridge. That place hasn't been built to make a couple of gadgets. That place is enormous. It is permanent. It is big enough to produce thousands. *Thousands*. What in hell for? Where are all our enemies? What are we afraid of? Why are we doing this?' Oppenheimer had no answer. 'You're right about one thing. If that thing works it is going to frighten the living shit out of everyone. And what does fear do to a man? It makes him anxious. Pretty soon everybody is going to want one. And then, boom! We've got a world full of Michael Merrimans, dying from the inside out. That's the future you're making for us. That's *our* future.' Shoenfield, worn out by his anger and fear, turned and stepped back into the entrance, then looked at Oppenheimer again. 'You've got to stop playing God,' he said gently. 'You're not good at it, and besides, the position is already taken.'

Around the tower at Trinity a cluster of tents rippled and billowed against the weather. They shrouded the gadget and a group of men, naked to their waists. Long, cold rivulets of sweat streaked down their backs as they laboured under the angry canvas. It was three in the afternoon and blisteringly hot. With the aid of a tiny dental mirror the core of plutonium was being slid gingerly into the heart of the beast. As it moved deeper, the Geiger counters rattled up in a crescendo. Then everything stopped.

'It's stuck.'

'Jesus Christ!'

'It must fit! We tested it on a dummy.' They pulled the core of plutonium out again and looked hard at the thing.

'The heat – it's so fuckin' hot, it's expanded.' They decided to allow time for the rest of the device to cook and expand.

'OK, let's try it again.' This time it slid home.

'It's ready,' someone whispered.

Oppenheimer walked from the hospital to his house on Bathtub Row. He entered the hall and slipped quietly into his study. When Kitty came in from the bedroom perhaps an hour later she discovered him sitting in his armchair, still soaked from the rain. A thick column of smoke curled up from his fingers. He swept the cigarette up to his mouth and sucked hard on it.

'Robert, you must get some sleep.'

'Once, when I was a kid on holiday, I tried to strangle a friend of mine.' He looked across to Kitty. 'He hadn't done anything. It was just this sudden fury.' Another deep lungful. 'Kitty, I'm in a very dark place.'

'I'll get you a sleeping pill.'

'I don't want to sleep.'

'Let me make you a drink then.'

'Kitty?' She stopped at the doorway. 'It's not just

our responsibility. We've all cooked this stew. The Germans, the British, the Japanese – the ugliness goes way back.' He was rambling, searching for some logic but failing to find any. Kitty could not follow. 'I'm not a scientist anymore, I'm a functionary.'

'You're not.'

'When I came here for the first time I didn't feel empty.'

Kitty searched for something to say but could find nothing. 'I know.'

'I know one thing, clear as a bell. I have got to stay in control. I have got to control who gets this thing.'

Kitty shook her head. Even to her ears, it sounded naïve. Suddenly she was angry. 'That's all you talk about, control and power.' She moved across to his side. 'Do you really believe you can control anything out here? What about the things you were good at? You know – life, the joy of living?' To Robert they sounded like old toys that had been lost somewhere in the back of the closet. 'Didn't you used to say that's what science ought to be about?' Her words were filled with grief.

'I know,' he mumbled, letting his head fall on to her breast.

'You have sacrificed everything to this.' Kitty moved to a chair, dragged it up before him and sat down. 'I put up with Jean because I thought you needed her. When I asked you to give her up – and you did – at first I thought it was for me. But it wasn't – it was for that *thing* – a thing she would have hated.' Robert heard her say aloud what he had always known. Like seeing a reflection in a mirror. 'I know I don't count . . .'

'It's not true,' he wanted to say, but he could only shake his head.

'Nothing counts for you except the bomb. That's all – your bomb. But it's not your only creation. Peter's so depressed you'd think he was in mourning. Toni doesn't know who you are – doesn't know what a father is.'

'Not so.'

'It is, my darling. I know you need my love and support. I *do* know that. But at the moment I'm all the children have.'

Robert leaned back in his chair, locked in his own misery, unable to see hers. 'Why me? Why did he pick me?'

The following morning, Saturday the 14th, broke against a pale, white sky. They all rose early out at Trinity and began the process of linking up the hoist chains. By mid-morning it was hot and humid. The slightest breath of wind lifted the perspiration from their faces and eased the strain. Oppenheimer had arrived just as the last of the chains had been attached and the winches were about to be tightened.

It was late morning before the motors were started. The tower let out a chorus of metallic complaints as the load was presented to it. Slowly, the gadget shifted. Out of its shroud-like tent the dark sphere emerged and began its hundred-foot climb towards the clouds. The chains clattered up through their pulleys and the great beast ascended. Festooned with wires and cables, it looked like a patient in intensive care.

In the distance, an unfocused peal of thunder rolled across the desert. The wind picked up a little and then it happened. A pulley suddenly parted from its joist, snapped in two and plummeted earthwards. It collided with joists along the way, ricocheting towards the gadget and then finally buried itself in the sand.

The gadget itself swung loose, dropped about a foot and then stopped, straining on the cables. On the ground they had all frozen – their worst fears racing for anyone to read across their faces. Oppenheimer felt he was keeping the thing in the air by sheer will-power. A tent flap crackled in the wind, the cables strained and then a voice said: 'It's fine. The safety's got her.'

SEVENTEEN

The day they finally hoisted the gadget to the top of the tower, Merriman slipped deeper into crisis. The heavens broke in the afternoon and another deluge descended on the desert. For those who were looking for signs, there were many, and they were all ominous. For those in security, the priorities were simple: button everything right up – tight.

The rain sheeted down against the hospital windows. Outside, the world had been transformed into a grey smear. Gutters overflowed, drains were blocked and a man with a newspaper over his head skittered across the road.

Shoenfield had forced the syringe deep into Merriman's chest and was searching for the wall of the heart.

'Pressure's falling fast,' announced the medic at his side. 'Got to get the fluid out now, Richard.'

'Here we go, Michael. Just me and you, pal.' Merriman was seated upright in a chair beside the empty bed. His head had grown in size and begun to blister. His eyes were two white spheres.

'OK, you're in. Now ease it out.' Slowly the syringe began to fill with fluid. 'Coming up slowly, it's coming up.'

*

By the late afternoon the wind had picked up. Thunder boomed around their heads, lightning snapped away over the horizon. A group of headlights appeared out of the driving rain and cruised up to the tents under the Trinity tower. Groves's door opened and he was out before the Buick had stopped. The general turned to the head of security.

'What's the big idea? They made a wrong turn and we've been all over the place.'

'Security idea, sir. Hear no evil . . .' But Groves was staring straight past him at the figure coming towards them, his arms waving above his head, his eyes blazing.

It was Oppenheimer. He was yelling through the rain. 'We've got to call a halt. This weather is impossible!'

Groves sighed and brushed the security man to one side. 'Forget it. We are *not* calling a halt because of the goddam weather.'

Oppenheimer stopped and waited as the general approached. 'No, you don't understand. The rain and wind. It'll dump radioactive material all the way from here to Amarillo.' Groves had passed him, forcing Oppenheimer to chase after him.

Groves was making for the accredited reporter from *The New York Times*.

'You the reporter?'

'Yes.'

'I want three reports . . .'

Oppenheimer had caught up with him. 'We've got 70,000 people there.'

'I want three reports,' Groves continued. 'One if we fail, one if we succeed and one if we disintegrate.'

The *Times* man hadn't understood a word. He looked at the frantic Egghead at Groves' side.

'No. I'm saying "no". We just can't do it. The weather's unpredictable. The whole picture's unstable.'

Groves turned on his man. 'The decision will be mine,' he said firmly, staring down the scientist. 'Right now, we go at 4 a.m. – and it stays that way!'

Oppenheimer was a statue in the driving rain. 'This is not a railway schedule we're planning here. You just don't understand.'

'Now you listen here. You're trying to un-invent this thing.' He jerked his thumb towards the top of the tower. 'But I can do this bit without you.'

'If you do – and I've said no . . .' The general waited for the rest. '. . . and something goes wrong . . .'

Suddenly there was a new player on the scene. Out of the rain emerged a bundled-up Fermi, soaked to the skin. 'Oppie, it's getting worse. The wind's impossible. Fallout will be uncontrollable . . .'

'I know, I know . . .'

Groves snatched Oppenheimer's arm and dragged him towards the car.

'Get in!' He signalled to the driver to take them away.

By the time night had fallen, the weather was still battling away outside. Kathleen had remained in the quarantined hallway, listening to the weather and watching everything collapse before her eyes. They hadn't turned the lights on because the place was meant to be deserted. When Shoenfield stepped into the hall it was a moment or two before he saw her.

'Kathleen, sweetheart, you've really got to go home. Get some rest.'

'I knew this thing had everybody in its grip. I should have stopped him. I didn't think I could.'

'Of course you couldn't.'

'I wish I could hold him.'

Shoenfield shifted his weight from one foot to the other. 'Do you think he'd even know I was there?'

'Sure. Of course he will.'

Oppenheimer and Groves were sitting in the car, separated by an abyss. The driver stared out ahead of him and switched on the headlights: 'The rain's stopped.'

Groves judged the moment was right. 'You build up to a moment, then you grab it. If not, it'll go right past you.'

Oppenheimer needed to escape from the general's overwhelming presence. He wrenched the door open and walked out into the wind. He felt the elements thrashing around him and he wondered what he could do.

There was the crunch of gravel behind. 'Why don't you just admit that you always wanted this . . . whatever.' Groves was looking at him sympathetically, paternally. After the long build-up Oppie needed some release.

'You never had any doubt, did you? That I'd do this . . . whatever.'

Groves stared out into the night. He saw no reason to answer. He had made his point and Oppie had – implicitly – agreed with him. But, 'What will it be like?'

'Unimaginable,' said the scientist softly.

Groves tried to conjure up the unimaginable. Knowing his point had gone home, he shrugged casually: 'OK, it's your baby.'

Oppenheimer turned to look at the man, but he was already heading back to the car. As he reached the door, Oppenheimer took a deep breath. Then: 'Do it.'

'Hallelujah,' whispered the general.

At the control centre Oppenheimer was handed a report. 'Winds aloft very light, variable to 40,000, surface calm, conditions holding for next two hours.'

Beneath the tower a small group sat beside the radio telephone. The wind was still buffeting the canvas, but was definitely weakening. Suddenly there was a burst of static over the RT. It was Oppenheimer.

'Prepare to fire at 0530 hours.'

'Roger. Roger.' Dennis Talmudge dropped the handset into its cradle. The 'old' physics professor from Harvard (he was nearly forty) had been given responsibility for directing the test. He stepped out of the tent and looked up into the tower.

Kistiakowsky had been stationed at the top. He had sat beside the gadget all the time they were waiting for the weather report. God knows what would have happened if it had been struck by lightning.

'Kisty?'

'Yes?'

'Proceed to arm.'

Beneath the tower they unlocked the padlock on a strong-box and lifted the lid. There were a series of heavy switches: OPEN, OPEN, OPEN, OPEN. One by one, Talmudge called out each circuit, Kisty checked them off and they were closed. The circuits were now live. Meanwhile, McDonald, his assistant, was throwing another set of switches and looking anxiously at the car. The circuits up to the control centre, 10,000 yards away, were functional. They prayed no one had left any controls on – or did anything until they were all as far away as possible.

In the quarantine ward the luminous hands on the clock showed a few minutes to five. Merriman's nerves had lost contact with his brain and his muscles were in spasm. He jerked and shivered. The life force was still present, but hopelessly trying to make sense out of the chaos within. Beside one dark, bloated arm was another figure, a head, resting on his hand. It was Kathleen. The hand jerked away and she took hold of it again.

'Easy, easy. I love you, Michael.' She guided the arm back towards the packed ice. 'Easy now, come on.'

Suddenly there were voices outside, the door swung open and the lights were snapped on.

'Christ!' Shoenfield and his colleagues had returned to make an inspection. 'Kathleen, what are you doing here? Come on, sweetheart.'

'I had to see him. I wanted to tell him . . .' They took hold of her and lifted her away from the bed. She started to weep as they swept her towards the door, as Merriman tried to lift himself from the pillow. There was a frozen, nightmare moment as he sat up. His hair remained on the pillow.

Then, 'Kathleen. Kathleen. Kathleen.'

She wrenched herself out of their grip and half-ran,

half-stumbled down the corridor towards the doors, out into the night where she let a scream escape from the very depths of her soul. It echoed across the roofs into the sky, a clear, cloudless sky, sparkling with stars.

Groves looked up at the sky and liked what he saw. An opening that would allow it all to come through.

'General?' Oppenheimer was waiting to escort him to the car that would take him to the observation centre.

Groves hesitated before he climbed in. Then he put a hand on Oppenheimer's shoulder, and said, 'I've always believed, truly believed, that the Lord was on our side. And now we're going to prove it.' He smiled the smile of a shy child.

At the top of the tower a sixty-watt bulb swung back and forth across the gadget. She looked just beautiful. In the distance a siren began its wail. At the Trinity base camp the siren was deafening. It had sent scores of people scurrying towards the trenches. Groves, now in his observation post, took a handful of suntan cream from a tub and smeared it on to his face. He looked up to see a green Very-Light rocket arc across the distant tower.

At Campana Hill overlooking the site, Enrico Fermi and Edward Teller watched the same green arc across the sky.

'Hey, Enrico. What do you bet the yield will be?'

'My bet is that we accidentally set fire to the atmosphere. If we're lucky, we'll only wipe out New

Mexico. If we can ignite the air, we'll finish off the planet. Any takers?'

Over the radio they heard the countdown: 'Zero minus one minute.' Then all of a sudden the shortwave Voice of America broadcast broke into their wavelength, playing the *Nutcracker Suite*. The operators desperately tried to clear the signal, but the piping clarinets stubbornly continued. Despite the distraction the well-drilled routine unrolled. Men lowered heavy welders' glasses and smeared themselves with thick white cream. They were no longer identifiable as individuals, but looked like members of some primitive tribe.

At the bunker 10,000 metres south of the tower, the lights on McDonald's control panel flickered on. Someone announced, 'Zero minus forty seconds.' The first bird of the dawn chorus started its song.

Underneath the tower, further panel lights began to glow. The needle on the firing unit swung violently to the right and the unit was fully energized. The *Nutcracker* drifted across the air and curled up the tower.

Back at South 10,000, the same evidence was displayed on a panel.

'Charging the device. The device is fully charged. Zero minus twenty.'

At base camp Groves growled about the music. Around him, men smeared in cream or shielded with goggles looked at each other and shrugged.

In South 10,000 the music had begun to mock them.

'Is this some kind of joke?' Kisty asked.

'Nothing we can do. It's a ground channel. They can't get rid of it.'

Someone looked across at Oppenheimer. His face was blank, his eyes on some distant object. Everything would happen automatically, he had nothing else to do but be there – and somehow he wasn't. Time had begun to stretch out. Kisty stepped up beside him and fumbled for a cigarette. Automatically Oppenheimer reached for his lighter but it was not there either. He felt an inexplicable panic rising. Kisty snapped a match and held it up to his cigarette, then offered it to Oppie. The flame illuminated the deep creases, the large open eyes now glazed. Something snuffed the match out, but the glow was still there. It was unreal. The glow increased until it had illuminated his entire face – and still it grew. Then it became dazzling. His face, the men around him, became translucent with light. A set of frozen figures, transfixed with a vision. Then the light began to penetrate their shields and burn into the retinas. Sharp, piercing pain. They looked away from the light, but then felt some invisible force, some divine hand – the shock wave – take them each by the throat and press their flesh hard against their bones.

Then the sound wave. A huge, grotesque, almost human laugh that roared up from the bowels of the earth towards the heavens. There before them all a demonic column of dust and debris reached higher and higher. It seemed to be alive. And no one could quite believe it. They had done it, and they were all sons of bitches now.

The news was flashed to Stimson, attending the Potsdam Conference, near Berlin. He quickly passed it to Truman.

OPERATED ON THIS MORNING. DIAGNOSIS NOT YET COMPLETE BUT RESULTS SEEM SATISFACTORY AND ALREADY EXCEED EXPECTATIONS.

The next day Truman marched into the conference hall and demanded that the Russians agree to allow democratic rights in the countries they had conquered in eastern Europe. The conference began in a mood of belligerence and ended in confusion. However, Truman came away with one absolute certainty. Stalin had confirmed that his armies would attack Japan during the first or second week of August. Before the Three Powers departed they issued a declaration demanding the Japanese surrender unconditionally. The declaration did not mention the forthcoming Russian attack. It did not mention the prospect of the atomic bomb, nor did it give the Japanese any reassurance about the future of the Emperor. The declaration was not signed by the Soviet Union.

The Japanese Government was confused by the declaration. On 28 July, at Arlington Hall, just outside of Washington DC, the US Signals Intelligence Service intercepted a coded Japanese message. The message stated that the Japanese government would not respond to the Potsdam Declaration until it could be more certain of Russia's intentions. Did the Soviets mean to join with their allies and declare war? The message begged for clarification. The Soviets refused to give it.

On 2 August Arlington Hall intercepted another message from the Japanese foreign minister. It was stunningly prophetic:

THE BATTLE SITUATION HAS BECOME ACUTE. THERE ARE ONLY A FEW DAYS LEFT IN WHICH TO MAKE ARRANGEMENTS TO END THE WAR. THE LOSS OF ONE DAY MAY RESULT IN A THOUSAND YEARS OF REGRET.

At 8.15 a.m. on Monday, 6 August 1945, the 'Little Boy' was dropped on Hiroshima. It killed 120,000 people.

On 8 August, exactly three months after the German defeat, Russian troops attacked Japan's armies in Manchuria.

At 11.02 a.m. on Thursday, 9 August 1945, 'Fat Man' was dropped on Nagasaki.

Altogether, over 200,000 people died here and at Hiroshima.

On 10 August the president received a message from the Japanese government offering to surrender.

Six days after the bomb was dropped on Nagasaki, Oppenheimer climbed into the back of an open jeep and was driven through the crowded streets of Los Alamos. The entire population had turned out – and they sent up a thunderous cry of joy and relief. Victory. Victory. It had been their victory – it was his victory.

From the back seat of his Buick Groves peered out at the scene. There was his man, his hands held together high above his head in celebration. He was watching the making of a legend. The stuff of *Time* and *Life* magazines. The hero, the conqueror, the shatterer of worlds.

Groves smiled.

Almost everyone was out there cheering, except for Kathleen and Richard. They had gathered up Michael's belongings – the diary, the baseball bat – and were leaving.

'We'll phone his dad from Santa Fe. Let him know I'm coming. The lines here are still . . .' She couldn't finish.

'Come on, sweetheart, we've got things to do.'

From the dorm they drove down to Shoenfield's lab to collect Babyface and lock the place up. They took the station-wagon out the main gate and took the road past the wild, rolling mesa. When they judged they were far enough away, Richard pulled over to the side of the road. He got out, walked round to the back and started to unload some wooden crates. From out of these came the animals from the lab. Rabbits, birds, racoons, dogs – soon the surrounding countryside was alive with creatures skittering off in every direction. It was a good thing to do, they thought. It was a good feeling to let things go free.

They could still hear the sounds of celebration in the distance. Oppenheimer was surrounded by praise and adulation. Yet his mind had turned back, back to an evening long before when he had come home and Kitty had been playing his old *Faust* recording. He thought of the scene at the end of Act I, where the philosopher Faust and the devil Mephistopheles sing a duet together, 'À moi les plaisirs' – ''Tis pleasure I covet'. Faust had just signed away his soul to the devil in return for unlimited wealth and power. The tenor and the bass harmonized together in a celebration that hinted at ultimate tragedy. Now somewhere, despite the successful test, despite the accolades, somewhere deep in the recesses of Oppenheimer's soul there remained the image of a man who had seen the face of evil – and had held its hand.

CODA

On Wednesday, 26 October 1949, a large dark sedan cruised down a neighbourhood street in San Francisco. It pulled up outside the Oppenheimer house and waited.

In the back yard, Oppenheimer had found himself a patch of early morning sunlight and settled into a garden chair. The children, Peter and Toni, were playing somewhere out of sight. Kitty came out from the house with a tea-tray.

'Groves will be here soon. I thought you could have tea out here.'

'Fine.'

'What does he want?'

Robert turned away and looked at the dew still glistening on the leaves. 'He wants to talk before I go to Washington tomorrow.'

Kitty sighed and looked across at the children. 'Should I take the kids inside?'

Robert nodded without looking up.

Groves, still feeling strange in his civilian clothes, although he had retired from the army nearly a year before, was led around to the back. He paused to take in the scene: Oppenheimer seated in a chair at the end of the garden, revelling in the sunlight. He waved to Groves, who waved back.

Groves refused tea and explained that this could only be a short visit. He watched Oppenheimer pour for himself and stir in a piece of lemon. 'I read –' he shifted in his seat – 'a letter of yours on Edward Teller's ideas.'

Oppenheimer sipped his tea. 'The Superbomb.'

'That's it.'

'I know why you're here.'

'If I remember correctly, you reckon that Teller's idea has caught the imagination of the military. The answer to Russia's bomb.' Oppenheimer nodded slowly. 'And yet you don't support it.'

'I know the research will, inevitably, be done.' Oppenheimer stirred his tea again. 'But I see no present need to produce the thing – even if it will work, which I doubt. And if we *do* go ahead and build it, well, I think it would be terribly irresponsible.'

'I'm not here to change your mind, Doctor.'

'Then why are you here?'

'I think you should know what the consequences might be.'

Oppenheimer looked hard at him for the first time. 'For the country?'

'For J. Robert Oppenheimer.'

There was another pause. Groves assumed Oppenheimer was taking the measure of his words. But instead he said, 'I hear you left the army. Westinghouse is it? Or DuPont?'

'The Remington Corporation.'

'The Remington Corporation,' Oppenheimer

echoed the words with mock enthusiasm. 'I never thought you'd leave the army. It must have been a hard decision.'

'Look, Doctor, I'm not here as someone's agent. I'm just here to explain things. From where I stood, you never seemed to understand much about the real world, the way things actually were.' Oppenheimer looked at him again, but now the arrogance was gone. 'Four months ago, that three-ring circus they call the House Un-American Activities Committee nailed your brother and his wife for being Communists. Yet everyone knows they left the Party long before he did any work for us. He was as loyal as I was. In fact, I even wrote him a reference. It didn't do him any good: he'll never work or teach again.'

'I can't see that Frank and I can be compared, really.'

'Don't imagine that you're impregnable. You're not. If those guys get up a head of steam, they'll come after you too. All they need is a reason.'

'My feelings about Teller's project are not political.'

'I know that.'

'Goddammit, I brought us to the edge.' The tranquillity had been punctured, his eyes were swimming. 'The Atomic Energy Commission will not recommend Teller's bomb.'

'If that's what happens, there are influential people in this business who will never forget it. They'll want to know why you put a halt to the project. They'll suspect foreign allegiances. More to the point, Robert, they'll cut you out and drop you. You've got to realize they have gathered mountains of stuff on you. They've got files this thick.' He held out his arms, a fisherman demonstrating his catch.

'I will *not* support Teller's bomb.'

'They'll call you a traitor. They'll bury you.'

'It's still no.'

Groves left it. The conversation was over. He had always known when there was no point in going further. He got to this feet and looked out across the lawn. 'When do you go to Washington?'

Oppenheimer put down his tea and stood up. 'Tomorrow night.' They walked back to the car together.

'You should know one thing. Whether or not you and the Atomic Energy Commission support the Super won't matter in the long run. They'll get their bomb eventually.'

'I know that. But they and the others who will listen will have heard Oppenheimer say no.'

A CHOICE OF PENGUIN FICTION

A Fanatic Heart Edna O'Brien

'A selection of twenty-nine stories (including four new ones) full of wit and feeling and savagery that prove that Edna O'Brien is one of the subtlest and most lavishly gifted writers we have' – A. Alvarez in the *Observer*

Charade John Mortimer

'Wonderful comedy . . . an almost Firbankian melancholy . . . John Mortimer's hero is helplessly English' – *Punch*. 'What is *Charade*? Comedy? Tragedy? Mystery? It is all three and more' – *Daily Express*

Casualties Lynne Reid Banks

'The plot grips; the prose is fast-moving and elegant; above all, the characters are wincingly, winningly human . . . if literary prizes were awarded for craftsmanship and emotional directness, *Casualties* would head the field' – *Daily Telegraph*

The Anatomy Lesson Philip Roth

The hilarious story of Nathan Zuckerman, the famous forty-year-old writer who decides to give it all up and become a doctor – and a pornographer – instead. 'The finest, boldest and funniest piece of fiction that Philip Roth has yet produced' – *Spectator*

Gabriel's Lament Paul Bailey

Shortlisted for the 1986 Booker Prize
'The best novel yet by one of the most careful fiction craftsmen of his generation' – *Guardian*. 'A magnificent novel, moving, eccentric and unforgettable. He has a rare feeling for language and an understanding of character which few can rival' – *Daily Telegraph*

Small Changes Marge Piercy

In the Sixties the world seemed to be making big changes – but for many women it was the small changes that were the hardest and the most profound. *Small Changes* is Marge Piercy's explosive new novel about women fighting to make their way in a man's world.